Candace squa̶ and glared at

'My reason for be̶ with you, Zac, and as long as I do my job properly it will continue to have nothing to do with you. OK?'

He was eyeing her thoughtfully, surprise still in his eyes, but the mouth was as forbidding as ever. She had come a long way since losing her sister, and Zachary Stephens wasn't going to spoil things now.

Dear Reader

March winds blow us good reading this month! Christine Adams' SMOOTH OPERATOR shows the useful as well as glamorous side of plastic surgery, while Drusilla Douglas has two sisters apparently after the same man in RIVALS FOR A SURGEON. Abigail Gordon's A DAUNTING DIVERSION is a touching story of a twin left alone to find a new path in life, and we welcome back Margaret Holt with AN INDISPENSABLE WOMAN. Enjoy!

The Editor

Abigail Gordon began writing some years ago at the suggestion of her sister, who is herself an established writer. She has found it an absorbing and fulfilling way of expressing herself, and feels that in the medical romance there is an opportunity to present realistically strong dramatic situations with which readers can identify. Abigail lives in a Cheshire village near Stockport, and is widowed with three grown up sons, and several grandchildren.

Recent titles by the same author:

CALMER WATERS
NO SHADOW OF DOUBT
JOEL'S WAY

A DAUNTING DIVERSION

BY

ABIGAIL GORDON

MILLS & BOON

MILLS & BOON LIMITED
ETON HOUSE, 18–24 PARADISE ROAD
RICHMOND, SURREY, TW9 1SR

MILLS & BOON, the Rose Device and LOVE ON CALL are trademarks of the publisher.

First published in Great Britain 1995
by Mills & Boon Limited

© Abigail Gordon 1995

Australian copyright 1995   Philippine copyright 1995
This edition 1995

ISBN 0 263 79000 2

Set in 10 on 11½ pt Linotron Times
03-9503-55864

Typeset in Great Britain by Centracet, Cambridge
Made and printed in Great Britain

CHAPTER ONE

CANDACE CARSON yawned as she paid off the taxi driver outside the Belgravia house, and as he drove away into the dark night she sauntered up the steps that led to an ornate pillared porch, trailing the white beaded jacket that went with her evening gown carelessly behind her.

A nearby church clock struck four as she fished for her keys and she shivered. It was two weeks to Christmas and there was a seasonal nip in the air.

The key kept missing the lock, and as Candace tried again, hiccuping softly as she did so, she knew that she was a little drunk. The champagne had been in plentiful supply at the pre-Christmas ball at the Dorchester and she'd drunk her share.

The key connected at last, and as the door swung open she gave a sigh of relief. For some reason her usual zest had been missing as she'd danced the night away at the glittering fund-raising event she'd just attended, and as she studied her face in the large mirror in the hall she wondered if she was losing her appetite for pleasure—or was it because Roddy was becoming a pain?

There were dark shadows beneath the violet eyes, and a disconsolate droop to the full curving lips, but the straight golden sheen of her hair and the delicate bone-structure beneath smooth skin that was still tanned from a month in Florida were enough to ensure that it was still a face to be remembered.

Roddy Carstairs was the latest in a line of indolent

5

socialisers to cast his eye on the attractive niece of Harry Carson, the industrialist, and like others before him he was in the process of discovering that Candace was a fish unwilling to be hooked. She was great company, liked a good time, and was on good terms with all the 'in' people, but that was it. If he'd read too much into a few casual embraces in the back of taxis, and her easy acceptance of his presence at the many social occasions that her privileged circle indulged in, he was going to have to think again, she'd decided in recent weeks.

Maybe she was just out of sorts, she thought as she went up to her suite on the first floor, and the prospect of driving north in the morning to attend Camilla's National Health Christmas party wasn't making her feel any better, even though it was always delightful to see her twin.

The girls had lost their parents in a yachting accident when they were twelve years old, and their only living relative, their father's brother, had taken them into his care. Uncle Harry was unmarried and spent most of his time jetting endlessly around the globe controlling his business enterprises.

He was kind and generous with the two orphans, but rather distant, finding himself out of his depth on his fleeting visits home, but he saw to it that they lacked for nothing in the new, strange life they'd been catapulted into.

Their parents had been reasonably well off, but it was as nothing compared to the wealth of Harry Carson that was always at the girls' disposal. The fact that their only confidants were the servants in those early days had been outweighed by the excitement of luxurious living, and Candace had soon developed a taste for pleasure.

To her amazement and dismay, Camilla, at eighteen,

had opted out of their cocooned lifestyle, and gone to train for nursing in the north of England. Now a qualified midwife, she was employed by a large hospital in a Cheshire town.

They weren't identical twins. Candace was a leggy natural blonde with a quick mind and an occasional short fuse, while Camilla, the quieter and more gentle of the two, was darker and smaller, but still with the same attractiveness as her sister.

The separation had hurt Candace deeply. They had been so close, and now weeks went by without them seeing each other. She acknowledged that they were equally to blame. For her part she invariably refused when Camilla invited her to stay in the basic little flat she'd found for herself, because it was cramped and dingy, and it annoyed her that her sister had turned down Harry's offer of superior accommodation. Added to that, hearing about the rigours of hospital life made Candace feel uneasy, guilty almost, and yet she'd told herself firmly she had no need to be. If Camilla had this obsession about being independent it didn't have to affect herself. *Her* life was easy and worry-free, and why shouldn't it be? It had been offered to her that way, so why refuse it?

Candace knew that Camilla worried about her 'aimless meanderings' as she described them, and when the subject came up she invariably retaliated with an at times unconvincing criticism of her sister's spartan existence.

When Camilla had phoned to ask her to be her guest at the hospital's Christmas party she had accepted, albeit reluctantly, as she was longing to see her twin, and as the young midwife rarely found time to come to London these days it was a case of the mountain having to go to Mahomet.

Her own Christmas programme was fully booked, tonight's function being the first of many, and she'd hoped that Camilla might be sharing some of them with her, but she was on duty all over Christmas, so it had been a vain hope.

Uncle Harry was due home from America on the morning of Christmas Eve, so at least she wouldn't be alone in the house with just the servants, a situation that wouldn't have bothered her at one time, but which now made her feel vaguely bereft. She had decided that if he wasn't too tired to venture forth into the whirl of festivities she'd planned she would like *him* to be her escort, in preference to Roddy or any of his ilk, and if that wasn't a sign of the awakening disenchantment inside her, she didn't know what was, she thought with a wry pout.

As Candace packed an overnight case the following morning, she hesitated over what to take with her for Montrose Hospital's big social event. She owned many expensive evening gowns, and as she eyed them thoughtfully it appeared that they might all be a bit over the top for the 'Bandager's Ball' as she'd wickedly described it to Camilla.

Yet why *shouldn't* she stun the northern folks? she reasoned. If her sister preferred theatre green to amber silk that wasn't *her* problem, and so the amber silk went in the case along with matching shoes and a heavy gold necklace and eardrops. The dress was elegant and flattering with its Grecian folds and revealing neckline, and the first time she'd worn it Roddy had exclaimed, 'Gee, Candace, you look like a goddess!'

She'd eyed him dispassionately. If the compliment had come from a man with a bit more backbone it might have made her heart beat faster, she'd thought as she led the way to the waiting taxi. But then who was *she* to talk about backbone?

There was a light covering of snow on the fields and hedgerows as she drove through the Cheshire countryside on the last few miles of her journey, and as she skirted the huge stone edifice of Montrose Hospital to get to the row of Edwardian houses where Camilla had her flat, its smooth lawns glistened white in a pale winter sun.

Her sister had just come off duty, and as they hugged each other in the pleasure of reunion Candace thought that Camilla looked pale and tired, and she thought, whimsically, that it was probably due to dancing attendance on mothers and babies, rather than jiving the night away at the Dorchester.

Camilla had left a meal prepared and as they ate it they exchanged news.

'Are you still seeing Roddy Carstairs?' Camilla wanted to know.

'Seeing. . .yes. . .seeing him in a different light! He bores me,' Candace said with a sigh. 'I'm beginning to think I've outgrown my yuppie friends.'

Camilla eyed her in amused mock amazement.

'I don't believe it! The belle of Belgravia is wearying of tinsel town!'

Candace gave her a playful push.

'Maybe, but I still haven't got to the stage where the Bandager's Ball is the highlight of my social calendar.'

Camilla laughed.

'You could be in for a surprise.'

'I doubt it,' she retorted with an answering smile, 'but to change the subject, tell me what's been happening in *your* life, apart from bedpans and the aforementioned bandages.'

Her sister's face was serious now.

'There's the other side of the coin, you know, Candace, like bringing babies into the world, along with all the hopes and fears that come with them, and the mothers of all shapes, sizes, and colours, some of whom are born to the task, while others haven't a clue.'

Candace wrinkled her small straight nose.

'Sounds messy.'

Camilla laughed.

'Not really. It's hard work, but exciting and fulfilling helping the next generation into the light of day.'

'If you say so,' Candace agreed languidly, ignoring a small pang of envy that was mischievously threatening to plague her. *She'd* brought up the subject and now she was ready to change it with all speed.

'What are you wearing at tonight's function?' she asked.

'The dark blue velvet Uncle Harry bought me last Christmas,' Camilla told her. 'And you?'

'An amber silk dress I had made in the autumn, and that reminds me: I'd better get it out of my case and hung up.'

As they cleared away the remains of the meal she said, 'You look pale, Camilla. Are you all right?'

'Yes, I'm fine,' Camilla assured her, 'just a bit tired, that's all. I think I might take a course of vitamins.'

'No men in your life, then?' Candace asked later as they dressed for the dinner dance.

Camilla flushed.

'I'm friendly with a couple of young doctors. . .one in particular. His name is Tom Makepeace.'

'I see,' Candace said meaningfully, 'and is this friendship leading anywhere?'

'No, not really. Tom's an Australian and due to go back home soon.'

'Brain drain?'

She laughed.

'Hardly. He's only recently qualified, and isn't specialising in anything at the moment. It's a case of his parents being unwell and him wanting to be near them. He came over here on a short-term exchange.'

'Too bad,' Candace consoled.

'Yes, too bad,' Camilla agreed with a smile.

The administration section of Montrose Hospital was in an old part of the building with high domed ceilings and ornate cornices. Polished wooden floors glowed beneath soft lights and a huge Christmas tree stood in the corner of the large foyer where the meal was to be served. A small stage had been erected at the far end, surrounded with hothouse plants from the hospital's greenhouses, and a thick red candle flickered on each windowsill.

Crisp white cloths bore the weight of heavy silver cutlery unflinchingly, and crystal glassware took on rainbow hues in the room's soft glow.

As Candace stood in the doorway with Camilla by her side they made a striking pair, the tall slender blonde in shimmering amber silk, with the heavy gold necklace lying flatly around her throat, and the loops that went with it swinging gently from her ears, while her sister, smaller, her hair caramel to Candace's silver fairness, and her pallor concealed beneath face-cream and blusher, made just as attractive a picture in dark blue velvet.

They weren't the only elegant women in the room, Candace noted. Some of the consultants' wives were wearing dresses that hadn't come off the peg, and the men scattered around were immaculate in dinner-jackets.

Camilla gave her a nudge.

'Well, what did I tell you?' It may not be the Guild Hall, but. . .'

'I'm impressed,' Candace whispered back, 'and becoming more impressed by the minute. Who's the Mel Gibson lookalike observing us from across the room?'

Camilla followed her glance and said with a smile, 'That's Tom's friend, Zachary Stephens, and don't let those stunning looks fool you. There's a rumour going around that he was born without a heart.'

Candace eyed her questioningly. 'Meaning?'

'He's invincible against all feminine wiles. The man's in love with his job, and has no time for anybody who isn't.'

Candace could still feel the dark unsmiling gaze directed at them, and unable to resist meeting it with her own, she murmured, 'He sounds a real bundle of fun.'

Camilla was smiling at a tall, rangy fair man who was ambling across towards them, and, her attention diverted from the sombre watcher, she said absently, 'Zac is Zac. . .a law unto himself, and Tom won't have a word said against him—and, talking of Tom, here he is.'

As Camilla introduced her to the young Australian, Candace dragged her eyes away from the man across the room, and as Tom Makepeace shook her hand warmly and gave her an easy smile it wasn't hard to decide which of Camilla's two doctor friends she preferred.

When it was announced that the meal was about to be served and would those present take their seats, Candace found herself next to Camilla with Tom Makepeace at the other side of her sister, and, as she glanced idly at the name card in front of the vacant seat next to herself, the morose spectator from the other side of the room was doing the same. 'Zachary Stephens', it said, and she stiffened.

'It would appear I have the pleasure,' he said unsmilingly in a flat northern voice as he settled himself beside her.

Candace eyed him coolly. If this was how he looked when he was having the pleasure she wouldn't like to see him when he wasn't, she thought edgily.

Camilla leaned forward and smiled at him. He smiled back, and watching him Candace thought how it softened the arrogant lines of his face. It was clear that he was on good terms with her sister, the warmth of the smile was proof of that.

'Hi, Zac,' Camilla said. 'Let me introduce my sister, Candace.'

The smile had gone, and, as he offered a lean brown hand for her to shake, Candace could feel the chill of his regard.

'Hello,' she said easily, placing her hand in his for the briefest of seconds, having no intention of letting him see how he was affecting her.

He nodded briefly, and then, unbelievably, said in the same flat tones, 'Camilla's told us a lot about you.'

She gave her sister a quick startled glance but Camilla was deep in conversation with Tom Makepeace, so there was no help coming from that direction.

'Really? That must have been interesting for you.' He wasn't the only one who could be aloof.

'Not particularly,' he told her with calm impudence. 'She obviously thinks you're the queen bee, but from what I've heard *your* place is with the drones.'

Anger brought the colour to her cheeks. How dared

he? The hard-eyed upstart! Criticising her before
they'd barely met!

'If your bedside manner is as tactful as your dinner
table conversation, you must be a riot on the wards,'
she said sweetly, and turning her head away she gave
the elderly man sitting opposite a dazzling smile. The
brusque young medic hadn't finished.

'She's always telling Tom and me what a classy sister
she's got, but then we've all got our own definitions of
"classy".' Amusement glinted for a brief second in the
hard eyes. 'What do they call you for short? Candy?
Sweet and brittle?'

No one, but no one, ever called her Candy, but this
odious creature would have to, wouldn't he? And not
only had he used the detested abbreviation of her
name, he'd managed to turn it into an insult as well!

The meal was going to be a nightmare with him
carping all the time, as it was obvious that Camilla and
Tom were absorbed in each other, but she'd coped
with bigger nuisances than Zachary Stephens in her
time, and so with the kind of smile that Camilla would
have known spelt trouble Candace began to fight back.

'Do tell me about *your* part of the hive,' she said
equally. 'Obviously *you're* one of the workers, but in
what respect?'

'I'm into obstetrics,' he said briefly, ignoring the
sarcasm. 'I've a long way to go but I intend to get
there. When I set out to do something I do it. It's a
part of medicine that has always fascinated me, though
I doubt I'll be found around the London clinics whenever *you* decide to start a family. I prefer to work in
deprived areas.'

'Yes, I thought you might,' she agreed blandly, 'and
as regards myself, I shan't be considering babies until
I've got a husband,' and with a quick sideways glance

at the dark profile beside her, 'and that could be in the distant future, as the selection isn't what it used to be.'

They were into the main course, and the man at her side was clearly enjoying the good wholesome food before him. No picking and piking with this one, she thought, and as if guessing what was in her mind he said, 'This is my first meal of the day.'

'Why is that?' she asked politely.

He sighed. 'Because there hasn't been time.'

Her eyes widened. 'You've been too busy to eat?'

'Yes.' And he went back to the enjoyment of his food.

As he ate, Candace was sizing him up. Dark brown hair in crisp waves was cut short around one of the most interesting faces she'd ever seen. She had glimpsed even white teeth inside an uncompromising mouth that looked as if it rarely smiled, and beneath the frown that seemed etched into his brow were wary dark eyes. It was a sombre face and yet an incredibly attractive one, and she thought it was a pity that such a stunning-looking man should have such a warped nature.

He didn't speak during the rest of the meal and Candace began to relax. At the first opportunity she would remove herself as far away as possible and maybe salvage some of the evening, but it didn't work out like that. She realised to her horror that they were meant to be a foursome.

'How dare you saddle me with this boorish individual?' she hissed in Camilla's ear when the two men were talking together.

Her sister laughed.

'Zac's a great guy when you get to know him, Candace. Brilliant at the job. He's going places, no doubt about it, and,' she added with a wicked twinkle, 'all the unattached females here are green with envy that you've got him for the evening.'

Candace glared at her.

'He may have the looks of a film star, but his manners leave a lot to be desired. Do you know he had the presumption to start ticking me off about my lifestyle?'

Camilla showed no surprise.

'Yes, he would. Zac thinks everyone should be as industrious as he.'

Candace snorted angrily.

'He's a pompous. . .'

She didn't get the chance to finish, as the pompous person in question was beside her, and, gesturing towards the floor that had been cleared for dancing, he said flatly, 'Shall we?'

She would like to dance, oh, yes, there was nothing she would like better. She was good at it, but then she *was* good at frivolous pursuits. That would be the next thing he would comment on. Well, he wasn't going to get the chance. A cool refusal was called for, but she wasn't quick enough. He was steering her on to the floor in the wake of Camilla and Tom, and before she knew it she was in his arms, and as they began to match their steps Candace saw without surprise that he was no mean performer.

The hostility seemed to have left him for the moment, and, as his arms tightened around her, the dismay she'd felt at such close contact with him disappeared. He danced as he behaved, strong and decisive, his hold firm and compelling, and her body obeyed his commands, so much so that when the music stopped and he released her she almost fell.

He moved away quickly without a backward glance and she stared after him angrily, until she saw the reason for his abrupt departure. Camilla was sagging in Tom Makepeace's arms, her eyes glazed, and her face deathly white.

By the time that Zachary Stephens had reached her sister, with Candace hot on his heels, a small group had congregated around them and her erstwhile dancing partner said tersely, 'Give her some air, please. She's fainted.'

He and Tom laid her gently on to the carpeting at the side of the dance-floor and the young Australian cradled Camilla's head in his lap. As he did so, she slowly opened her eyes and to Candace's immense relief the glazed look had gone.

'What happened?' she asked weakly.

Candace took her hand and it was very warm.

'You fainted,' she said gently.

Zachary Stephens was looming over them.

'I suggest we take her home,' he said abruptly.

Candace nodded. Those who had been aware of Camilla's collapse had gone back to their dancing when she'd opened her eyes, but one of the consultants remained, an elderly man with his smartly dressed wife beside him, and as he felt Camilla's pulse he said to the two young doctors, 'Keep an eye on her. The pulse is a bit slow. It seems to be merely a faint, but one rarely faints without reason,' and to Camilla who was struggling to her feet, 'You'd better take it easy, young woman. A check-up would do no harm.'

Candace was blaming herself for not taking more notice of her sister's pallor and signs of exhaustion, and as they took her back to the flat she was remembering how when they were young Camilla would rather drop in her tracks than admit that she wasn't well, and it looked as if nothing had changed, she thought anxiously.

When they'd settled her on to the sofa Zac said, 'Is there any brandy in the flat, Camilla?'

'In the kitchen cupboard,' she said weakly.

He came striding in with a small glass in his hand seconds later, and said gently, 'Drink this, Milla, and don't frighten us like that again!'

It was clear that the tough nut had a soft kernel when it came to her sister, Candace thought. . .and he'd used her own pet name for her. She wondered what the lanky Australian thought about the extent of Zac's concern. Nothing untoward, it would appear, as he was smiling down on them in benign approval, and when Zac said, 'I think old Benson was right. A few days off the wards would do you no harm,' Tom nodded his agreement.

Watching them, Candace thought these three were in harmony. Their work in health care provided a mutual bond, and they shared an easy camaraderie. *She* was the only discordant note—the pleasure-seeker, the outsider.

They stayed for a while, and when both were satisfied that Camilla appeared no worse from her earlier brief collapse they took their leave, with Zachary Stephens once more reiterating that rest and a check-up for Camilla wouldn't be a bad idea.

'And that is *something* coming from Zac,' Tom told Candace with a laugh. 'Because *he* is indefatigable, he cracks the whip over the rest of us.'

Candace eyed the man in question coldly. He'd redeemed himself in part through his concern for Camilla, but she hadn't forgotten his insulting castigation of herself, and if it weren't for the fact that she was decidedly uneasy about her sister she would have been grateful that Camilla's moment of weakness had rescued her from his clutches.

After they had gone Candace began to question her.

'Has this happened before?'

'No.'

'Do you feel ill?'

'I've felt better. I'm very tired and my head aches terribly.'

'How long have you been feeling unwell?'

'A couple of weeks. . .ever since I was laid low for a few days with some sort of virus.'

'Some sort of virus!' Candace exclaimed. 'You work in a hospital and you don't know what's wrong with you when you're ill!'

Camilla smiled weakly.

'I work with babies. . .not in the path lab.'

Candace was not to be put off. 'Did anyone examine you?'

'No, there was no cause. I just stayed in bed.'

'And no doubt went back to work before you should.'

She saw that Camilla was beginning to shiver, and when Candace felt her forehead it was burning, and yet her hands that had been so warm, were now icy cold. Panic gripped her. They'd let the two young doctors go and now it was starting to look as if it hadn't just been a faint. She was breathing rapidly and the glazed look was back in her eyes, and as Candace stood over her helplessly, she lost consciousness again.

Candace flew to the phone and dialled emergency, and as she waited for the ambulance service to reply there was a frightening feeling of unreality inside her. The girl on the couch breathing so fast, and lapsing in and out of consciousness, was Camilla, the nurse who knew all about illness, unflappable, efficient Camilla, while she, Candace, the drone, to quote her caustic companion of what seemed a lifetime ago, was in charge, and petrified at the thought.

A crash team was waiting at Montrose Casualty when they arrived and the duty doctor's face was grave as he examined her.

'What's the pulse like?' he asked of the nurse assisting him.

'Weak, but rapid,' was the reply.

He was touching Camilla's hands and feet.

'Extremities very cold,' he commented. 'Check the blood-pressure.'

When she had finished, her gravity matched his.

'Much reduced.'

'Right,' he barked. 'Get Mr Fitzgerald.'

Candace, watching in frozen anguish, saw the nurse hesitate, and her eyes widened when the girl said, 'He's at the dinner dance.'

The dance! It was still in progress! She checked her watch and thought raggedly that it was only a couple of hours since they'd left.

'I don't care if he's dining with the Queen,' the harassed doctor shouted. 'Get him!'

At some time during the night Tom Makepeace and Zachary Stephens appeared beside Candace as she sat mutely in the waiting-room. The young Australian's face was grave, but his companion's expression gave nothing away. It was closed and unreadable as before, but even in her anxiety she could sense some sort of angry turbulence inside him.

The consultant who'd been brought from the dance-floor had hinted at septic shock, and when it had been explained to Candace in laymen's terms she'd gone cold with fear.

An X-ray had shown there to be an abscess in

Camilla's lung from which bacteria appeared to have multiplied to a dangerous level, bringing about a life threatening condition.

'We won't be able to confirm that it *is* septic shock until we've identified the bacteria from the organisms from the blood sample we've taken,' he told her. 'In the meantime, I've arranged immediate treatment in the form of antibiotic injections, and a transfusion of fluid replacement to combat signs of kidney failure. We're also going to administer intravenous infusions and oxygen therapy in an attempt to raise the blood-pressure.'

As she'd tried to absorb what he was telling her he'd said with a sympathetic smile, 'And on top of all that, once I've changed into my theatre clothes I'm going to remove what we believe is the source of the infection. . .in this case, the abscess. She's very ill I'm afraid, Miss Carson,' he'd told her soberly. 'I would say that your sister has been run-down for some time, and that the illness that attacked her recently was some form of pneumonia which left pus in the lung forming an abscess. We're doing everything possible, but I have to stress that the situation is very serious, as septic shock attacks the body from all sides.'

'I thought it was only associated with tampons,' she'd said questioningly and he'd shaken his head.

'No, my dear. There are many causes, such as urinary tract infections, gastroenteritis, cancer, pneumonia and its complications. All of them can create an infection from which bacteria multiplies. In your sister's case, it would appear to be the abscess secreted in the lung.'

In the days that followed, Camilla's two doctor friends presented themselves in the intensive care unit whenever they had a free moment. Zachary Stephens, in particular, seemed to be calling in all the time, but not in the role of comforter, she thought wretchedly. His face was grim, the dark eyes full of frustration, and she was even more convinced that he loved Camilla.

If it *was* so, he wasn't admitting it, but then his type never confessed to ordinary weaknesses, she concluded bitterly. Her own limp misery must be a constant source of irritation to him.

Uncle Harry had flown in from America in reply to her agitated phone call, and when the burly grey-haired businessman had arrived at Montrose, Candace had at last felt there was someone of her own to support her.

He'd booked into an hotel and tried to persuade her to join him there, instead of staying in Camilla's dismal flat, but she'd refused. Candace had felt that Camilla would want her to be there, filling her place in the empty rooms, and as it comforted her to be surrounded by her sister's things she'd stayed put.

Harry Carson was deeply concerned about both his nieces. He wasn't a demonstrative man, but in his own way he was very fond of the two pretty orphans he'd taken under his wing, and although his anxiety was much greater with regard to Camilla, he was also very worried about the pale-faced shell that was his other niece, the pleasure-loving, indolent Candace. He felt helpless because it was a situation where all the money in the world wouldn't put things right for them.

Camilla died on Christmas Eve. Candace and Harry were with her, and as his broad shoulders shook with grief he saw that the girl at the other side of the bed was tearless.

They had been warned that the end could come any time and had never left her side, but now Candace got to her feet and pushed her hair back wearily. She stood looking down on her sister and then bent and kissed the thin cheek gently.

'There's nothing here for us now,' she told her uncle tonelessly. 'Shall we go?'

Harry nodded mutely as he wiped his eyes, and as Candace led the way into the corridor, she almost collided with the man gazing bleakly out of the window.

When he turned, Zachary Stephens said in harsh grief, 'They've just told me. What a waste that it should be *her* to go. Camilla, with so much to live for, so caring and dedicated, so needed.'

Candace eyed him stonily.

'I presume that the point you're trying to make is, why wasn't it somebody who won't be missed. . .like me. . .the drone.' And, taking her uncle's arm, she walked past him without a backward glance.

CHAPTER TWO

YEARS later, when Candace thought back to that time, it was as if the Christmas and New Year had never been. The only significant event of the festive season had been Camilla's funeral, and after that one grey day had followed another.

It had taken her until the spring to acknowledge what was in her mind, and when she'd brought the vague stirrings of purpose out into the open it was as if she'd known all along that she was going to follow in Camilla's steps, not so much as in taking her place, but going into health care. . .into nursing. It was a frightening thought, but she didn't have to search her heart for reasons.

There was the memory, crystal-clear as it always would be, of those anguished days at Montrose Hospital while Camilla was fighting for her life. Candace had seen the round-the-clock care her sister had received from doctors and nurses working tirelessly against one of nature's vicious quirks, and it had made her realise why Camilla had been prepared to cast off the shackles of idle living for a life that had purpose. For the first time in her life, Candace had experienced humility.

All of that had been reason enough for her decision, but above all else was the desire to prove her own worth. The memory of dark scornful eyes in an arresting face, weighing her up and finding her lacking, *and* not hesitating to say so, was never far away. Zachary Stephens hadn't been short of nerve, and even now she

bridled at his censure, but she also admitted that he'd
been right. She'd been put on the earth for more than
pleasure.

They'd met just once since, in the period between
that black Christmas and the spring. Tom Makepeace
had called on her in London before flying home to
Australia, and, clinging to any link with Camilla, she'd
driven him to the airport, only to find that someone
else was there to see him off. He'd been standing by
the book stall, idly leafing through a magazine, and as
he'd swung round in answer to Tom's call, his amazement had matched hers.

'Well, if it isn't Candy!' he'd said in the voice that
seemed to be forever in her ears, its tone unchanged,
flat, northern, and disparaging.

Tom had grinned at them both.

'I'm going to get a paperback. I'll leave you two to
get reacquainted.'

Candace had wondered if she would ever see him
again, so that she might discover if her detestation of
him was as strong, strong enough to cancel out the
quickening of her pulses.

In jeans and a sweatshirt, with old trainers on his
feet, he'd looked no different from any other English
male in his late twenties, until her eyes sought his face
and then it was different, every line of it was fixed in
her memory, none of it connected with gladness, and
as she met his challenging gaze she saw that nothing
had changed.

He was still the most attractive man she'd ever met.
Beside him, the rest of his sex were pale and indistinct,
but her loathing was still there. When she'd been at
her lowest ebb, he'd offered her criticism instead of
comfort, disdain instead of kindness, and she wasn't
going to forget, even though she was aware that she in

turn had fallen victim to a malady, not of the body, but the mind, and the name of the virus that seemed to be forever in her blood was Zachary Stephens.

'Hello, Zac,' she said coldly, her thoughts rocketing around in her head. 'I wasn't expecting to see *you* here. You've actually taken a day off work.'

'Tom's not the only one who's leaving Montrose behind,' he'd told her in his abrupt fashion. '*I* finished yesterday, too, and am off to pastures new.'

'I see,' she'd said slowly, wondering where his fresh grazing grounds were to be, and determined not to ask.

'How are you?' he'd asked.

'Coping,' she'd told him quietly. 'Trying to come to terms with a bereavement, and only those who've had to do it know what it means.'

'Yes. Though I'm afraid *I* wouldn't know,' he'd said offhandedly. 'I haven't anyone to grieve over.'

She'd stared at him puzzled, and, as Tom came back to join them at that moment, enlightenment was denied her.

She could have said goodbye to the Australian then and left them together, but for some reason Candace hadn't done. Whether it was because she'd wanted to prolong the moment with her castigator, or was still grasping at contact with anyone who'd known Camilla, she didn't know, but she'd waited, and they saw Tom off together.

There was silence between them when he'd gone striding off to the waiting aircraft, and if it hadn't seemed so unlikely she'd have thought that Zachary Stephens was unsure of himself, as some men were in her presence, but not Mr Bumptious, she'd thought grimly, never him.

'Care for a coffee?' he'd asked brusquely, and, taken by surprise, she'd said,

'Er. . .yes. . .thank you.'

Candace had seated herself at a table in the airport lounge and watched him covertly as he queued at the counter. Why was he so abrupt? she wondered. It couldn't be just that he thought her idle, surely? There must be some other reason for his abrasiveness, and if there was, she wasn't likely to discover what it was, as this meeting was a one-off as far as *she* was concerned, and as for Zac it must be stretching his civility to the limit having coffee with her.

'Still painting the town red?' he asked as they sipped the hot liquid.

Candace might have told him she could have painted it with tears. She'd shed enough since Camilla died, but he wouldn't want to hear that. . .it spelt of weakness, and so she said tartly, 'It's a wonder you don't walk with a limp, the size of the chip on your shoulder. Getting back to your remark about not having anyone to grieve over, I should have realised that *you* weren't born. . .you must have been chiselled.'

As she'd got to her feet and picked up her bag and gloves she'd seen an expression on his face that had almost stopped her in her tracks. . .but not quite.

'Thanks for the coffee,' she'd said stonily, and walked away with a long casual stride.

And now the wheel had turned its full circle. After two years in Project 2000, attached to a London hospital, where her training had consisted of a month on the wards and a month in school alternately, Candace had opted to spend a further period training for midwifery as Camilla had done, and, once she was qualified, had applied for a position at Montrose Hospital in the maternity unit.

Almost four years after the events that had changed

her life she was as happy as she'd been in a long time, and when her application was accepted it made it all seem worthwhile.

When she'd told her uncle of her plans in the barren spring after Camilla's death, he'd eyed her in dismay. His beautiful niece was still attractive but drooping sadly, and he'd made a point of being with her at every opportunity that his business commitments would allow.

'There's no need to punish yourself like this, child,' Harry Carson had said gently. 'How do you know you're cut out for the job?'

She'd smiled a twisted smile.

'I don't, do I? But I can adjust. I'll have to. . .and I'm going to.'

He'd still been unconvinced.

'Camilla wouldn't want this,' he'd persisted.

Candace had smiled naturally for the first time in weeks.

'I think she would, Uncle Harry. She never approved of my lack of direction.'

He'd shaken his head anxiously.

'Well, it's up to you, my dear, but I feel that you ought to wait a while. I don't want you to make a mistake. You've had enough to bear in the last few months.'

He'd eyed her thoughtfully.

'This hasn't anything to do with that dark young doctor, I don't recall his name, who couldn't take his eyes off you, has it?'

'No, it hasn't. That is if you mean the one who hadn't a good word to say to me. He's someone I'd rather forget.' If only it were that easy, she'd thought.

* * *

The training had been hard and tiring, and in the first few months Candace had rubbed her aching back and soaked her feet and wished she'd taken her uncle's advice, but as the days went by she'd adjusted, and been amazed to find how interesting and rewarding the work was.

Her decision to go into midwifery hadn't been entirely connected with Camilla. She'd had to do a stint in all the various wards during her training and had found maternity to be the most fascinating, so much so that she'd decided to specialise, and for reasons that *were* connected with her sister had opted to do it at Montrose.

In the last few days before moving north to continue the career that not so long ago would have seemed as improbable as a walk on the moon, Candace was beginning to have doubts about the wisdom of going back to the place were Camilla had worked, a place that held such sad memories. Time had made the scars of grief less jagged, but she knew it wouldn't take much to gouge them open again, and kept asking herself if she was making a mistake. However, the compulsion was strong and when the big stone building of Montrose Hospital appeared on the skyline on a warm June morning the panic inside her subsided and peace took its place.

'I'm here, Milla,' she whispered, 'and it's where I want to be. . .need to be. I know you understand.'

Kate Summers was in charge of the midwifery section and when the newest member of her team presented herself at her office, she sighed. The fine-boned, long-legged blonde with the shadowed blue eyes was a surprise, and she eyed her thoughtfully. This one didn't look as if she would have much stamina. She had plenty of style, but it wasn't style they were looking for on the baby unit, it was skill and energy, and an ability to fit in with the rest of them.

The girl wasn't much younger than herself, but any similarity ended there. Kate was plain, plump and pleasant, just as long as no one impinged on the efficiency she demanded from the staff on the unit. If that should occur, the tyrant in her surfaced and it was woe betide the culprit.

Unmarried, Kate lived with her widowed mother who worked as a doctor's receptionist, and when she wasn't at Montrose the two of them enjoyed a busy social life away from their medical backgrounds.

Mary Summers would have liked to see her daughter married and with babies of her own, instead of spending her life delivering the children of others, and it grieved her that the men around didn't see beneath her daughter's plain exterior to the quality beneath.

'Leave it, Mum,' Kate would say with a smile when Mary grew restive at her unmarried state. 'I'm in no rush to tie myself down. My work at Montrose comes first.' And she meant it. The job was everything to Kate Summers, and now, on a busy Monday morning, she'd been presented with the most glamorous offering that the Health Service had ever allocated to Maternity.

'Never judge a sausage by its skin, Katie,' her grandad used to tell her when she was small, and if ever there was an occasion for remembering the old adage it was now, she thought, as she surveyed the golden girl.

Candace was getting restive beneath the other woman's regard, and then Kate Summers smiled.

'Welcome to the three Ms,' she said, and, as Candace

stared at her in perplexity, 'Montrose Maternity Madhouse.'

The newcomer laughed. 'Ah, I see. Thank you for that. I'm looking forward to joining you.'

Kate nodded, hoping that the pleasure wasn't going to be all one-sided.

'Good,' she said briskly. 'We've a happy team here and I hope you will settle in with us all right.'

Was there a note of doubt in her voice? Candace wondered, but there wasn't time to dwell on the thought, as her plain-faced senior was asking, 'Are you familiar with Montrose?'

She saw that Candace's face had changed colour, the honey skin had whitened and her mouth had formed into a tight bud.

'I was here in a visiting capacity some years ago, but I've heard nothing of the hospital since.'

Kate had been glancing at the information she'd been given about the new staff nurse and her head came up at the toneless reply to her question.

'I suppose that's not really surprising. You're from southern England, aren't you?'

Candace nodded.

'More or less,' she said. She could have added that since losing Camilla she hadn't felt as if she belonged anywhere. She'd been a piece of flotsam that had reached out blindly for an anchorage, and hopefully was going to find it at Montrose Hospital.

It would seem that Kate Summers hadn't been there in Camilla's time or the name Carson would have rung a bell, and for that Candace was thankful. The less known about her, the easier it would be to keep a check on her emotions.

When she was introduced to the rest of the staff on Maternity she found a variance in their attitudes. A young auxiliary called Tracey weighed her up with huge envious eyes, and of the two other staff nurses, both in their thirties, who like herself must have done the extra eighteen months training demanded by the UK Central Council on Midwifery, one of them, a pretty West Indian by the name of Lala, shook her firmly by the hand, while the other, a small girl with sharp eyes and a button mouth, merely nodded.

'We have three obstetricians on the unit,' Kate Summers explained as they moved towards where a plump middle-aged man with limp brown hair was emerging from behind the curtains around one of the beds. She nodded in his direction, 'That's Gordon Grampion. He's one of them. I'll introduce you,' and as Candace shook a hand that was as limp as the hair she was aware that the plump man was eyeing her with more than passing interest.

When he'd moved on to the next bed, Kate said, 'Rowland Ashley is the top guy, and Grampion and his colleague, who is the favourite with staff and patients alike, and on leave at present, are the heirs to the throne.'

She was propelling Candace through swing doors into a room where alterations were in progress, and she said, 'This is, or will be, what the staff have named the "lagoon room", or to be more circumspect the "birthing pool". There are so many mothers wanting to have their babies in a birthing tank these days, and so Montrose is out to accommodate them.'

Candace was frowning. She'd had experience of the system in the London hospital where she'd trained, and was aware that some babies had suffered ear damage in the process.

Kate Summers was watching her.

'Yes, I know there's a government enquiry pending.

These new ideas are introduced and they're not always successful, I'm afraid.'

'Like birthing stools?' Candace said.

The other woman laughed.

'Yes, no doubt they'll be the next,' she said drily, and as they went back on to the wards, 'Take it slowly, Candace Carson. No matter how experienced we are, a new environment is always unsettling at first.' She smiled and it transformed her homely face. 'But I'm sure that by the end of the week you'll feel as if you've been here forever.'

Candace could have told her that she'd already felt like that with regard to Montrose Hospital, as the memory of what had seemed like endless days and nights came painfully back to mind, but she pushed it away and, her eyes lightening, said quietly, 'I'm sure that you're right about that, and as you've just suggested I'll feel my way at first. . .and thanks for showing me round.'

'My pleasure,' was the reply, 'and now I'm going to leave you with Lala and Debbie, and remember I'm here if you have any problems.'

'And where do *you* live?' the sharp faced Debbie asked when their senior had gone.

'I'm normally based in London,' Candace told her, 'and will probably spend my free time there, but for the time that I'm here I've rented an apartment at College Lawns by the university.'

'Very smart!' the other woman exclaimed with a trace of acidity. 'If you can afford to live there, you shouldn't need to work for your living.'

Candace eyed her thoughtfully. This one was going to be a thorn, but it was early days to judge and so she said serenely, 'My need to work is not connected with my financial status,' and with a smile for Lala, who had been evincing some dismay at her colleague's asperity, she said, 'Perhaps you'd like to put me in the picture regarding the patients.'

It appeared that most of the mothers in the two wards had given birth normally and were on the standard twenty-four-hour stay, but two of them had experienced difficulties and their babies had been in the neonatal unit, one of them still incubated.

Lala explained that Jane Bowen, a primigravada in her early forties, had been admitted in a state of premature labour with a dilation of five centimetres on arrival. She had been given an epidural anaesthetic and the baby had been born a couple of hours later with the aid of forceps. Fortunately Baby Bowen, at thirty-two weeks' gestation, was in quite good condition and was transferred to the neonatal unit. At the present time she was incubated on an apnoea mattress and had been having milk feeds of two millilitres per hour along with donated breast milk at longer intervals.

'She was doing fine until this morning,' the West Indian nurse said in a low voice as they passed the mother's bed, 'but a low-grade fever has developed and she's been vomiting, which means we've had to stop the feeding and put her on gentamicin and fludoxacillin. Hopefully it will be just a minor set-back. Gordon Grampion has seen her and will be keeping her under observation.'

As they crossed the corridor into the second and smaller maternity ward, Lala nodded to where a pretty copper-haired girl was coming out of the bathroom, walking slowly with a towel and sponge bag over her arm.

'That's Tamsin Jones,' she said. 'Her baby was in the neonatal unit but he's with her now. She'd started in normal labour but progress was very slow, and towards the end of the first stage the baby became distressed. A vacuum extraction didn't work, and it ended in a difficult forceps delivery which gave us a limp, pale, full-term baby that didn't appear to be breathing. It was just one on the apgar score and so we intubated with all speed.'

'And what then?' Candace asked. She'd come across asphyxia at birth during her training and was interested to see what the routine was at Montrose.

'The endotracheal tube was connected to the oxygen supply which had a pressure-limiting valve, and a T piece occlusion with a finger over the end of the tube gave us ventilation of twenty breaths a minute. Needless to say during all this the mother was frantic, but we were soon able to reassure her as the heartbeat increased steadily, though it *was* a few minutes before he started breathing on his own. Obviously we'll be keeping a close watch on Baby Jones, but so far, so good.'

And so it had gone on, with Candace finding her way on that first day, and all the time with a feeling of unreality. Her 'aimless wanderings', as Camilla had described them, were over, had been ever since she'd enrolled as a trainee nurse, and there were no regrets in her, only the determination to prove to herself that she *wasn't* useless, and if the strength of it was still connected with the scorn in a pair of dark eyes, it didn't matter any more. Zachary Stephens was long since gone from Montrose Hospital and she wasn't going to complain about that.

By the end of two weeks Candace *did* feel as if she'd always been part of the big friendly hospital. The work was hard but gratifying, the tiny new arrivals delightful, and the mothers an interesting though mixed bunch.

She rang Uncle Harry a couple of times, and

although he no longer had any worries about his
beautiful niece he was glad to receive her assurances
that all was well and that she was happy. It was true,
she was, and amazingly it was because her life had
done an about-turn. Her socialising had taken a back
seat, in fact it was almost non-existent, and her work,
all-enveloping, totally absorbing, had taken over, and
for now it was enough. She was walking a different
path, and with every step moving towards a different
kind of maturity.

It was the Monday morning of her third week at
Montrose, and as Candace inspected herself in the long
mirror in her bedroom she was reasonably satisfied
with what she saw. The image was no longer that of a
pleasure-loving yuppie. The smooth skin and fine bone-
structure were unchanged, but the eyes were more
guarded, the mouth more purposeful, and in the deep
blue uniform there was a new efficiency about her.

She'd braided her hair into a golden plait and coiled
it around her head, and she thought wryly that it was
the only part of her that was 'goddess'-like these days.
Roddy would have a fit if he knew what she was up to,
but he was another who was long since gone from her
life, and there were definitely no regrets on *that* score.

There had been a big intake over the weekend and
the moment Candace presented herself on the unit it
was all systems go. When she went into the labour
ward, Debbie was already there and she said dourly,
'Seems as if you and I are in here today, and we've got
a problem.' She indicated a bed at the end of the room
from where there was coming a loud wailing sound. 'A
hysterical and uncooperative single mother,' she
announced, 'who turns a deaf ear to any form of
counselling.'

'How far on is she?' Candace asked, eyeing the wriggling hump under the bedclothes.

'Just faint contractions, but somebody brought her here and just dumped her.'

'How old is she?'

'Nineteen. . .and she's got diabetes.'

'Gestational?'

'Yes. She's had to diet and needed insulin. The obstetrician has seen her every week since her glucola level showed diabetes, and she clings to him like a limpet.'

'Poor kid,' Candace said softly. 'Is there a father around?'

'Not shown himself so far, neither have her parents, if she has any.'

'A case for adoption?'

'Possibly, although it's not been mentioned.'

There was a high-pitched howl from the bed and Candace hurried to the girl's side.

'Are the contractions speeding up?' she asked gently.

'No, they're not!' the girl hissed. 'Go away! I want my doctor! Where is he? Why doesn't he come?'

'Shush, he'll be here soon,' she said comfortingly, while wondering if Gordon Grampion was on the unit, or the rarely seen Rowland Ashley. In the half-hour since she had come on duty there hadn't been a sign of either.

Candace checked the report left by the obstetrics nurse who had seen her during the night and noted that the uterine contractions were mild and spasmodic, that the bag of waters was intact, and that the patient had last eaten at nine o'clock the previous evening, and as if to give emphasis to that fact, she shouted, 'I'm hungry! Don't they feed you in this place?'

Frizzed brown hair was splayed over the pillow and

smudged frightened eyes glared at Candace as she observed her. The girl's name was Kerry Maddox, and normally she would be classed as small, but not at this moment. She was huge.

Candace was aware that in a diabetic pregnant mother there was often an excess of amniotic fluid around the foetus. It was not normally a threat to the mother but could lead to complications during delivery, and doctors usually preferred to bring the foetus a little earlier as it was often large.

In Kerry's case, she was at thirty-six weeks' gestation and showing signs of labour, but in view of the irregularity of the contractions and their non-progressive element, it was possibly a false alarm, gas in the bowel or something similar.

Candace lifted her nightgown and began to listen to the foetus, and as she did so the girl lashed out with her arm and sent her crashing backwards into the arms of the man who had come up behind her, and was in the act of drawing the curtains around the bed.

'Careful!' he cautioned as he caught her, and Candace froze. She couldn't see his face. She had her back to him, but the voice was enough. Its scolding tones had haunted her dreams more times than she cared to admit.

She shrugged herself out his hold and turned round slowly, pulling her skirt straight with one hand and rearranging her cap with the other.

His face stretched.

'Candy!' he breathed. 'What are *you* doing here?' and then before she could answer, 'Don't tell me. Let me guess.' He gave a hard laugh. 'It's because you like the uniform. . .and blue suits you.'

Coming from anyone else that would have made her laugh, but not from him. He was as stunning as ever, and just as caustic, she thought, in that moment of meeting, and what in the name of heaven was he doing at Montrose?

She hadn't spoken so far, but it didn't seem to be bothering him.

'The last person I would have expected to see on my first day back from leave is. . .'

'The drone?' she interrupted tonelessly as her mind grappled with the fact that the holidaying obstetrician and everybody's chum was Zachary Stephens.

That day at the airport he had said that he was leaving Montrose, and it had never occurred to her to check if he had come back. If she had done so, it was a certain fact that she wouldn't be here.

She squared her shoulders and glared at him.

'My reason for being here is nothing to do with you, Zac, and as long as I do my job properly it will continue to have nothing to do with you. OK?'

He was eyeing her thoughtfully, surprise still in his eyes, but the mouth was as forbidding as ever. Candace knew that, having started off on the wrong foot with him all those years ago, through no fault of her own, it wasn't going to be easy to behave as if they were just colleagues in the normal sense of the word, but she was going to have a good try. She had come a long way since losing Camilla, and Zachary Stephens wasn't going to spoil things now.

'It's *me* you should be talking to, Doctor, not *her*,' the girl on the bed cried fretfully, and immediately his attention switched to her, and with a gentleness that Candace wouldn't have believed possible he said, 'Hello, Kerry. Now what's this about one of my favourite patients starting to have her baby almost before I'm back from holiday?'

As Candace stood beside them stiffly the girl said plaintively, 'You promised you'd be here.'

'And here I am,' he announced. 'And I'm going to do something about all the discomfort you're in.'

CHAPTER THREE

'AND how is the glamorous newcomer shaping up?' Mary Summers had asked of her daughter on Sunday afternoon.

Kate had smiled.

'Excellent,' she said generously. 'Candace Carson is an asset to the unit. I had my doubts about her at first, as you know. She looked too decorative to be useful, but it isn't so. As is often said about beauty with brains, she isn't just a pretty face, even though Gordon Grampion can't take his eyes off her. She's keen without being pushy, confident but not cocky, and good with the patients, so what more could I ask?'

'Is she married?' Mary had asked.

'Not as far as I know. She doesn't wear a ring. Candace is very reticent about her private life. Certainly no man has been mentioned, which is strange; with those looks you'd expect them to be queueing up.'

'How many times have I told you that beauty is only skin-deep?' Mary had reminded her and Kate had begun to laugh.

'They'll have to peel *me* like a grape then, if they want to find it.'

Her mother had patted her arm gently.

'Get away with you,' she'd said softly, and then, going back to the previous topic, 'Why don't you invite her round for a meal? They're a stuck-up lot at College Lawns. I'll bet she doesn't know a soul. . .in a strange town and with no obvious family around her. Roast beef and my Yorkshire pudding, with a good helping of spotted dick to follow, will give her an idea of our northern hospitality.'

Kate had given her slim dark haired mother a playful push.

'You're only looking for praise, and, knowing you, if Candace likes your Yorkshire pudding you'll be her friend for life.'

Mary had smiled.

'Not if she starts snaffling all the unattached men.'

Kate had become suddenly serious.

'I don't somehow think she will,' she'd said thoughtfully, 'and talking about men who're fancy-free, Zac's back tomorrow, and nobody, staff and patients alike, will be complaining about that. He's a gem, especially so when one has to put up with Gordon floundering around, or having to bow the knee to the great Rowland.'

'Rowland Ashley is a nice man,' Mary had protested. 'If he seems withdrawn and not easy to communicate with, it's hardly surprising as he's still shattered at losing Janine.'

'Yes, I suppose he is,' Kate had agreed, averting her eyes from her mother's candid gaze, 'but from the way she behaved you would have thought he would have known there would be a tragedy sooner or later.'

'He probably did,' Mary had acknowledged, 'but no matter how much we love someone, it's not always easy to divert them from a collision course.'

There had been silence between them then until Kate had got to her feet and said in a lighter tone, 'As you've been bragging about our wholesome northern food, Mum, what's for tea?'

Mary had laughed.

'Beans on toast? Salad? Omelette?' and as Kate had

groaned in exaggerated dismay, 'It's too warm for roast beef.'

And now on Monday morning Zachary Stephens was back and looking much more relaxed than when he'd left for a badly needed holiday two weeks previously.

Kate was content. Zac got things done. *He* wasn't shut away in an ivory tower like Rowland Ashley, or bumbling around like Gordon. He was meticulous, efficient and tireless, and if at times too withdrew into sombre reserve the staff put up with it because of his exccllence.

When he'd called into her office, she had asked him if he'd enjoyed the break, and he'd replied, 'Yes, if it could be described as that.' When she had eyed him in puzzlement, he'd given his guarded smile and said, 'I've been back to my roots, Kate.' Before she could ask what he meant he'd gone striding off to see the teenage girl that he had been monitoring all through her pregnancy.

Her peace of mind was short-lived. Within minutes of Zac's departure, Candace Carson had come out of the labour ward as white as a sheet, and when Kate had got up from her desk and slowly followed her to the nurse's rest-room she'd found her gazing bleakly out of the window.

'Is anything wrong?' Kate asked.

Candace swung around. The answer to that question was yes. Everything was wrong. Zachary Stephens was here, entrenched at Montrose, and the satisfaction and confidence she had felt before setting out that morning had ebbed away, but she could hardly tell her likeable superior that. Kate would lose confidence in her then. Nor was she going to tell her that they were acquainted, and that he had never said a pleasant word to her. . . and it hurt.

Instead, she dragged up a smile and told Kate, 'I've got a bad headache, that's all. I just needed a moment alone.'

The other woman eyed her shrewdly. If she was telling the truth, sick staff were not efficient staff, but Lala was absent due to a bereavement, and if she sent Candace home they would be seriously short-staffed.

'I don't need to go home,' Candace assured her, reading her thoughts. 'I feel better already.'

'You're sure?' she questioned.

'Yes, thanks,' Candace said quietly, and wondered why she wasn't saying the words that were hovering on her lips, words that would be painful to say, but in light of the morning's events sensible and necessary—in effect that she wanted to hand in her notice.

When she got back to the labour ward Zac had gone and she breathed a sigh of relief. Those moments beside Kerry Maddox's bed had been too traumatic for a repeat so soon, and while he was out of the way she was going to pull herself together. It was incredible that he was back at Montrose, and that they would be seeing each other constantly on the Maternity Unit. She supposed she should blame herself for coming to this place above all others, but it had never occurred to her that she might find him here.

'Zac Stephens has calmed our hysterical young friend down,' Debbie announced, 'and the rest of our ladies in labour are feeling the benefit. It only needs one like that to upset the lot, and he knows it. He's seen her frequently during her pregnancy because of the diabetes, and he appeared just at the right moment, but then he always does.'

'Not as far as I'm concerned,' Candace said unthinkingly, and Debbie's sharp eyes glinted.

'You know him?'

'We're acquainted. . .yes, from a long time ago,' Candace admitted reluctantly.

'Socially?'

'No, nothing like that,' she said hastily, wishing she had watched her tongue, but then who was to say that *Zac* wouldn't tell the folks here who she was, that they had met before, and he hadn't been impressed.

'I thought he looked a bit stunned when he was sorting young Kerry out. It must have been the shock of seeing a face from the past,' Debbie commented.

'I doubt it,' Candace said drily, having recovered her poise. 'There's not much that would put Zachary Stephens off his stride.'

'You're probably right,' the other conceded. 'He's a tough one, but they don't come any better.'

So he even had the redoubtable Debbie eating out of his hand, Candace thought as she went to check the contractions of a new arrival. The dark, smouldering type must be flavour of the month at Montrose, but then it would appear that he knew his job, excelled at it, and who was she to question that?

He was back. She sensed it before she could see him. Maybe it was because Debbie was actually smiling, or perhaps it was because the patient she was examining was straining to see around her extended stomach.

Candace kept her head down. If she could make herself inconspicuous he might spare her any further turmoil. It was a vain hope. His footsteps were coming towards her, and, when they stopped, her downward glance was fixed on the hem of his surgical coat and the feet planted firmly beside her on the polished floor.

'I'm going to perform a Caesarean section on Kerry Maddox this afternoon,' he said briefly. 'I shall require you to assist. OK?'

No, it wasn't, but she wasn't going to tell him so.

'Yes, of course,' she said calmly, and hoped that she was the only one who could hear the thudding of her heart.

'Are you sure that you and Zac aren't matey?' Debbie asked curiously when he had gone.

'Positive,' Candace told her firmly as her mind tried to grapple with the afternoon's daunting prospect.

Zac was in front of her in the queue in the cafeteria at lunchtime, laughing and chatting with those on either side of him and, watching him, Candace marvelled. Was this the same man who had been prepared to condemn her because she didn't match up to his standards? It would appear that Zachary Stephens had many faces. He had been tender with Camilla and the girl in the labour ward, but there had never been any niceness left over for her.

In spite of his apparent good humour, Zac took his meal to an empty table and proceeded to tuck into the food, and Candace, having observed his position, was careful to steer clear by going round the back of him once she had been served.

As she was putting her tray down on the table, he swung round and their eyes met, and she knew he had been aware of her presence. He half rose from his seat and for an agonising moment she thought he was about to join her. In a panic she sat down quickly, bent her head over the plate, and started to eat.

It worked. He turned back to his table, and Candace thought grimly that if ever there was a recipe for indigestion it was having to share a meal with the thinking man's Scrooge.

He hadn't given up on her, though. When she went into the hospital gardens for the last few minutes of her lunch hour she discovered him close behind, and as she turned to face him he said abruptly, 'So why *are* you here at Montrose?'

No pleasant small talk, no welcome or bonhomie, just a bald question, and she thought that while he might have been on the front row when they were giving out the looks, he had surely been back of the queue when it came to manners.

How would he react if she told him the truth? That he had been right about her uselessness, and that meeting *him*, and at the same time losing Camilla, had changed her life. She could visualise the dark brows rising in disbelief and the strong mouth curving in disdain, and didn't want to have to watch *that*. In point of fact she didn't want to answer the question at all, but it was as if her natural assertiveness disappeared when Zachary Stephens was around, and she found herself answering flatly, 'I fancied a change of scene.'

He was the last person she was going to tell about all the heart-searching she had done before moving into health care, and of the hard graft that had brought her to midwifery at Montrose.

At her flippant reply, something flickered in his eyes and it wasn't disbelief or disdain. It was an emotion she couldn't identify.

'Where did you train?' he asked.

'London.'

She saw no reason to go into any further details.

'I see.'

'I don't think you do!' she flared. 'You're too blink-ered with your own ideas.'

He took a deep breath, and stepping forward gripped her by the forearms.

'Why *did* you come into nursing, Candace?' he grated. 'Was it because of Camilla. . .or me. . .or for some other reason?'

'You!' she hooted. 'If I'd known I was going to find you here, I'd have done the fastest about-turn in the memory of man.'

'Woman,' he corrected with a dangerous smile, and her colour rose. His hands were still on her arms, not hurtfully on her smooth skin, but neither was his grip loose. It was a restraining hold, and for the second time in an hour there was panic inside her. Zac was stopping her from moving away, making her stand close and subservient, and she couldn't make the effort to throw off his grip and depart. Her body felt weak and languorous, yet her heartbeats were like thunder in her ears.

There was a gleam in his eyes and she knew that he was as affected by the moment as she, but was it in the same way?

She was to find out. He was using the grasp on her arms to draw her to him, and when their eyes were level and their mouths almost touching he said in his flat northern voice, 'It's not a game, you know, Candace.'

She stared at him.

'What? What's not a game?'

'This. . .us. . .Montrose.'

Now she *did* have the strength to fling him off. How dared he even think she saw it as a game? A large chunk of her life with lots of pain and grief *and* discomfort woven into it had gone into bringing her to this place, and he had the cheek to call it a game. Or had she misunderstood him? What had he meant when he'd said *us*? There was certainly no game being played between *them*. A battle of wits. . .or wills, maybe, but not a game, unless he meant the pull of the sexes, and if that was what he was pontificating about, she might as well give him something to think about.

She flung herself out of his grasp, and as his arms

slid away it was her turn to take hold of him. As she embraced him his lips parted in surprise and she placed her mouth on his and kissed him long and sensuously.

For the first few seconds, amazement had him frozen into stillness and then he responded with a ferocity that rocked her on her feet.

Candace had been kissed before, many times, but nothing had prepared her for this. As they clung together everything else receded, pushed back by the passion that gripped them, and then she was moving away from him, and with the back of her hand against her bruised lips she gasped recklessly, 'Is that the sort of game you mean?'

Zac shook his head.

'I don't play games with other people's emotions, though it would seem that *you* do.'

'Oh, no?' she challenged, as the full realisation of what had just occurred hit her. 'You're a past master at it!'

A large floral clock beside them said that there were three minutes of her lunch hour left.

'I must go,' she said quickly. 'I'll see you in Theatre.'

He eyed her consideringly.

'Yes, you surely will,' he said, and it was hard to tell if it was a threat or a promise.

Candace had assisted at Caesarean sections before and not been especially apprehensive, until today, and even now it wasn't the procedure that was alarming her. . . it was the main participant, and the thought that he would be watching to see if she made a wrong move. But the moment she went into Theatre her worries disappeared. Personal problems and intrusive vibes became microscopic at these times. A new life was soon to be brought into the world, and for the young girl about to be anaesthetised nothing would ever be the same again.

Candace hoped there would be someone to support her, that she wasn't going to be giving the baby up for adoption, or having to carry the burden of caring for it alone, as so many young mothers were having to do.

Her own maternal yearnings had surfaced of late. It hadn't been until she had assisted at her first delivery that the wonder of producing a tiny human being of one's own had hit her, and she'd been choked with awe as she had witnessed the infant's arrival and the subsequent joy of the mother. It was perhaps only then that she'd understood the reason for Camilla's commitment to infant care and a surly young doctor's dedication. And now that same doctor was back in her life, and if hospital routine was anything to go by he would be occupying a large slice of it.

As she stepped into the role of scrub nurse, Candace was so conscious of his presence that she felt lightheaded. Was it only minutes ago that they had been in each other's arms beside the floral clock?

Their glances held above the surgical masks, hers bright, blue, and questioning, his guarded and watchful, but there was no time to talk. It was time for the operation to begin.

A catheter had been inserted to empty the bladder. The amniotic fluid around the baby had been suctioned off, and Zac was ready to make the midline vertical incision that was necessary because Kerry's large baby was in transverse position with its shoulder in the birth canal.

She had been given a general anaesthetic, as Zac had thought that any of the sensations still present during a regional one could bring on a recurrence of the girl's hysteria and that wouldn't help either mother or baby.

As they worked together, Candace's movements were deft and confident, anticipating his wishes, responding instantly to his commands, grateful that in one thing at least they were in tune.

If she'd dared, or had the time to dwell on what had happened between them earlier, she might have decided there was another area where they'd found harmony. . .sexual harmony. And at one time that would have been enough, but not now, not with *this* man. She wanted more: his approval, his time, his life spent with her, and if her hand faltered for the merest second it was because of another birth. . .the birth of her love for Zachary Stephens.

The baby, a healthy-looking boy, had been delivered through the incision in Kerry's stomach, the umbilical cord cut and the afterbirth removed, and when the entries into the abdomen and uterus had been closed up Kerry was to be given an injection of ergometrine which would help the uterus to go back into position and prevent bleeding.

'The scar won't be below bikini height, I'm afraid,' Zac said as he scrubbed off, 'but that's a minor detail as far as I'm concerned. Kerry's got a sturdy-looking lad there. Let's hope she has the sense to do what's right by him.'

'That's always in the lap of the gods, isn't it?' she said.

'Yes, it is,' he agreed sombrely, 'and those who bring a child into the world only to discard it are incredibly cruel.'

It wasn't a casual comment. Candace could tell that. It came from deep within him, and she had a desperate urge to know why.

'Do I take it that your last remark came from experience?' she asked quietly.

He was drying his hands, and when he turned to face her she'd already worked out the answer.

'Yes, it did. *I* was dumped within days of being born, and no matter how caring the facilities are for the abandoned child the feeling of limbo is always there.'

'So you were never adopted?'

'No. Lots of folk looked me over, but mustn't have liked what they saw.'

'But you must have been an attractive child?' she said.

He laughed, and it was the first natural expression of mirth she had seen from him.

'I was also an awkward little monster.'

'I can believe *that*,' she said, joining in his laughter.

Zac paused as he was about to depart, leaving the mother and baby in her care, with the assistance of a young nurse from the maternity ward who had performed in a secondary capacity.

'I thought we worked well together,' he said as she eyed him questioningly, and on that surprising statement he went.

As Candace let herself into the apartment that night she was smiling. The day that had started off so traumatically had thrown off its gloom and brought happiness. She had broken through Zac's reserve. Hadn't she just! His response to her tantalising kiss had been such that she felt as if the memory of his mouth on hers would be with her forever, and then, even more amazingly if that were possible, he had thrown her a crumb of praise, and the delight she'd felt at that was indescribable. She thought happily that maybe working with Zac was going to be the best thing that had ever happened to her, instead of the worst.

She was too hyped-up to eat, and after a leisurely

bath she slipped on a rose silk kimono and went to sit in her small garden.

Children's voices drifted over from the nearby fields, and birds chirped in the sun-drenched trees, and with the scent of flowers around her Candace closed her eyes and let her mind go back to that other garden, huge, well-kept, the scene of her mid-day meeting with Zac. As she relived every second of that devastating kiss she knew that, just as today had altered Kerry's life forever, so it had altered hers.

She was in love with a man who was virtually a stranger, sombre, reserved, and living with the hurt of rejection forever inside him, and her mouth curved tenderly as she thought how she'd like to make it up to him, to be a buffer against the pain that always had him on the defensive.

She'd known from the start that there was something else bugging him as well as his impatience with her lifestyle, and now, unbelievably, he'd told her what it was. It must be a strange feeling for Zac on the occasions when he delivered babies that might end up the same as he, she thought, and his patience with Kerry and her like must come from pain remembered.

The light went at last as the sun slipped below the skyline and the warm silence of a summer night fell over the garden. Candace got to her feet. She was hungry now, and the thought of a sandwich and a glass of wine was appealing, but there were footsteps on the path, and as she peered into the gloom a proud head and wide shoulders were outlined against the night sky.

'Candace?' he said.

'Zac!' she breathed as pleasure swept over her with the certainty that *he* must have been thinking on the same lines as she, but he wasn't alone. A woman stepped from behind him in the shadows and when she spoke Candace knew that Montrose Hospital was well represented at that precise moment.

'Hello there,' Kate Summers said. 'I hope we're not intruding.'

'No, of course not,' she assured her quickly. 'What can I do for you?'

'You can accept an invitation to dinner on Saturday night if you will,' Kate said with a smile. 'It comes courtesy of Mum and me, and we'd love to have you. It would be a welcome to the bustling north sort of occasion. Zac will be there and a couple of other folks.'

She was wearing a white flowered sun-dress with a matching headband, and her pleasant face was happy and relaxed, while Zac looked trim and very appetising in a white towelling shirt and khaki shorts. Candace pulled the kimono more tightly around her. Her long legs were exposed at the bottom, the smooth skin of her neck at the top, and her breasts thrusting against its smooth silk. They both looked so cool and right for the warm night, while she felt like a geisha girl!

'I'd love to,' she said, acutely aware of Zac standing silently beside the young nursing manager. What were these two doing together? she asked herself. Were they a couple? It would hurt a lot if they were.

Kate smiled.

'Lovely. We're so glad you'll come, aren't we, Zac?'

He nodded.

'Yes.'

The monosyllable was neither gushing nor unfriendly, just an answer to a question, and her earlier happiness began to dwindle. She was angry with herself. What was the matter with her? She had been around long enough to know that a kiss didn't mean a ring on one's finger, and if it did, that was the last thing most women wanted these days.

'We'll get along, then,' Kate said easily, and with a glance around her, 'What a very nice place you've got here, Candace.'

'Yes, it's not bad,' she agreed. Compared to her usual dwelling places it was mediocre. Uncle Harry had three houses and they were all sumptuous, but, knowing Zac, he probably thought that this was over-the-top enough.

'Goodnight, Candy,' he said as Kate led the way out of the garden, 'and make sure that you lock up.'

She stared after their departing figures, her mind full of questions. That had been a strange thing to say. He'd almost sounded concerned about her, and what was all this 'we' whenever Kate referred to him? And he was back to calling her 'Candy'.

Candace saw Zac several times during the rest of the week and on each occasion there was a state of guarded truce between them, which manifested itself in a polite rapport that was a far cry from those moments in each other's arms in the hospital gardens.

If *he* remembered the brief scorching seconds of passion they had shared he gave no sign of it. He was back to his grave, industrious self, and if Candace found it incredible that he could blot it out of his mind so easily, she was equally amazed that he'd told her about his deprived childhood in those few intimate moments after Kerry Maddox's Caesarean section. It had been two gigantic steps forward in their relationship in one day, but when he'd appeared with Kate that night in the summer twilight it had seemed like an even bigger step backwards.

She found herself watching how often he went into Kate's office, and whenever she saw a white-coated figure in there, it was a relief when it turned out to be one of the other obstetricians.

Rowland Ashley, who was senior among them, was a quiet, fair man of medium height in his early forties, who had lost his wife in a car crash some twelve months previously, and been left with a small boy to bring up. From what Candace could make out from the hospital gossip, she'd had a drink problem and had taken the car out when not fit to drive. Fortunately Henry, their son, hadn't been with her, or he might have suffered a similar fate. Rowland had apparently adored his party-loving wife and was still traumatised by what had happened. His problems had increased the workload for his two assistants, with Zac taking it in his stride, and the limp Gordon continuing at his normal slow pace.

Candace had decided that Gordon Grampion mightn't be the most motivated medic she'd ever met, but he was no sloth when it came to the pursuit of a pretty face, and at the present time hers was the one he was after.

'That one is a ladies' man,' Lala had informed her after he had waylaid Candace on the ward several times. 'They say he has already had the one wife, and she got tired of his eyeing others.'

Candace had smiled. She could handle men like Gordon Grampion. It was when they came in the mould of Zachary Stephens that she wasn't so sure.

On the Friday afternoon one of the nursery nurses noticed that a baby born to an Asian mother was rather sleepy, not feeding well, and looked jaundiced. The obstetrician was sent for and when Zac came striding in Candace breathed a sigh of relief. She'd seen enough of 'groping Gordon' as he was known to the staff for one week, and not nearly enough of his busy counterpart.

He smiled at her briefly as he went to examine the infant, and when he came out of the nursery he said, 'I've requested that the bilirubin level be checked, and if it's as high as I think it might be it's physiological jaundice, and phototherapy will have to be started.'

He glanced around the labour ward where, for once, there was normal progression and no stress.

'Everything all right with you?'

'Me personally. . .or the job?' she questioned.

His eyes met hers, dark and unreadable as always.

'The job, of course.'

'Yes, fine,' she said coolly, annoyed with herself for making him state the obvious.

'Good. You're going to Kate's dinner-party, then?'

'Yes, I think so.'

She had been having second thoughts about her rash acceptance of the invitation, but knew she was going to go, even if it did mean an evening of misery fending off Gordon, and watching Kate and Zac displaying the closeness they had shown the other night.

CHAPTER FOUR

CANDACE didn't have to spend the evening fending off Gordon Grampion, because he wasn't a guest at Kate's little dinner party, and she wondered why she had been taking it for granted he would be there. Maybe it was because she was expecting it to be a gathering of medical folk for some reason, and on that assumption she wasn't far out.

Rowland Ashley was there, looking livelier than of late, and John Airdrie, the elderly GP that Mary Summers worked for, along with another of his receptionists, Betty Barclay, a plump motherly-looking lady. Then there was an old school friend of Kate's, Judith Grant, a district nurse, who'd brought along her new husband, which called for congratulations all round. . . and then there was Zac, looking relaxed and good humoured for once in a black polo neck sweater and grey trousers.

He appeared to be in the same kind of mood as the other night when he and Kate had appeared in her garden, and Candace thought that perhaps the other woman had that kind of effect on him, whereas *she* seemed to bring forth either fire or brimstone.

There were four men, four women, and their hostess, to whom Candace had taken an instant liking. Mary Summers was a pleasant and attractive woman, who clearly had a good relationship with her daughter, and watching them together, Candace had felt a tug of sadness. She'd been denied the loving bonding between mother and daughter that strengthens in adult life, as

58

Camilla and herself had been barely twelve when they lost their parents. They'd been lucky to have each other, but now Camilla was gone too, and Candace hadn't had a serious relationship with anyone of either sex since.

There had been no desire in her for it, and renewing her acquaintance with Zachary Stephens had made her realise why. Critical he might have been, still was for that matter, and abrasive and sarcastic to name but a few of the characteristics that had made her fume, but he was the only man she'd ever given a second thought to. . .and three. . .and four. . .and five. . .

And now he was watching her over the top of a sherry glass as she was being introduced to Mary's grizzled employer, and when the elderly GP said genially, 'Now this young lady isn't one of us, surely? If I had to guess I'd say she was an actress. . .or a model,' Candace found herself watching for Zac's reaction.

It came with an ironic raising of his glass, and as her colour deepened she told John with a laugh and a defiant toss of her golden head, 'Something much more exciting than that. . .I'm an obstetrics nurse. . .a midwife.'

'You are!' he exclaimed. 'You're one of Kate's lot?'

'Yes, I am.'

'Well, I'll be blowed! So out of the lot of us here, four of you are in the baby business?'

'It would appear so.'

When they sat down for the meal, Zac was across the table from her with Kate sandwiched between him and Rowland Ashley. Every time Candace looked up his eyes were on her, and she wished that just for once she could read his thoughts. If she could see respect or admiration in his dark glance she would be happy, deliriously so, but that would be like asking for the moon, and there was no chance of anyone climbing up into the sky to get *that* for her.

John Airdrie was seated next to her and following her glance he said on a more serious note, 'Our young obstetrician looks well tonight. I'm continually having to tell him to slow down.'

She eyed him in alarm.

'He's not ill, is he?'

He laughed.

'No, of course not. They don't come any fitter, which is just as well, the way he drives himself.' He eyed her curiously. 'Would it have mattered if he had been?'

Of course it would, she thought painfully. Three people held her heart. One of them, Camilla, was gone, wiped out by a rare condition. Uncle Harry, as far as she knew, was fit and well, and she hoped he would stay that way, and the third, though he'd no doubt be amazed to know it, was Zac, and in a moment of complete selflessness Candace knew she could endure anything other than that any harm should come to him.

It *had* been roast beef with Yorkshire pudding on the menu, but not the threatened spotted dick; instead they'd had a delightful pavlova for dessert, and when they gathered in the Summers' small sitting-room for coffee Candace found Zac by her side.

'Were you and John discussing me?' he asked in his usual forthright manner.

She smiled.

'Yes. He was saying you looked well tonight, but that you drive yourself too hard.'

He laughed and it was amazing how it transformed his attractive face.

'John's an old fusspot. I keep telling him I'm in my prime.'

Oh, you're in your prime all right, she thought as she took in the trim physique and the strong, capable hands. In your prime physically and mentally too, except for that small area of the mind that has been fenced off through deprivation.

Unaware of her deliberations, he said, 'It's no wonder John thought you belonged to the arts. You make everyone else here look so ordinary.'

Not *you*, Zac, she wanted to say. Never *you*!

She looked down at the plain black silk dress she'd chosen to wear with the sapphire necklace that Uncle Harry had given her last Christmas, and wondered why he couldn't have just paid her a normal compliment, instead of turning it into a veiled reprimand.

'I'm not sure whether to take that as a compliment or not,' she told him coolly, 'but if past experience is anything to go by I don't think I should.'

His mouth curved in brief amusement and she longed to kiss it again.

'I wouldn't have thought you that short on compliments that you have to rely on *me*. There isn't a man here who can take his eyes off you.'

Her mouth went dry. Was he admitting that *he* wasn't immune to her either? Whatever his meaning, she wasn't going to let him see that it mattered one way or the other, and so she said sweetly, 'Not Rowland Ashley. He's only got eyes for Kate.'

That had him off balance. He swung round to observe the lady in question and saw that she and his superior were indeed engrossed in each other, but he shrugged it off with a casual. 'He'll be telling her his troubles. Rowland is a fine doctor, but he's not much use at punching life on the nose when it goes for him.'

'And *you* are, I suppose?'

He gave a hard laugh.

'What do *you* think, Candy? I've had to fight every inch of the way.'

She had a sudden vision of a small boy with dark curls and a bonny face, who'd learnt painfully that a surly sort of aggressiveness could become an armour against life's deficiencies.

'Milla and I lost our parents when we were twelve,' she said softly.

He stared at her.

'I didn't know. She never said.'

'There was no point in making a big deal of it, was there? We were lucky, Uncle Harry stepped in and took us in hand.'

'So you think *I* make a big deal of it?' he asked in a low voice. 'Well, it may surprise you to know that you're the only person I've ever discussed my life with.'

It was her turn to be surprised.

'You haven't told Kate?'

'No. Why should I?'

'I don't know. Why should you, I suppose,' she said faintly as she tried to take in the fact that he had confided his background to her alone.

When everyone was ready to depart into a warm moonlit night Candace asked, 'Can I give anyone a lift?'

She wasn't expecting to be taken up on the offer as it looked as if everyone had come by car, but to her surprise Zac said, 'Yes, me. I walked across, but, as I have a long day ahead of me tomorrow, a lift home is appealing.'

'You're not working, surely!' Kate exclaimed. 'Not on a Sunday—that's what we have the relief staff for.'

He shook his head.

'No. Not work in that sense of the word.'

When he was seated beside her Candace asked, 'Where do you live, Zac?'

It seemed incredible that she was in love with a man and wasn't even aware of where he lived.

He smiled, and without thinking she said jokingly, 'You'll have to watch it or it will become a habit.'

Zac stared at her blankly.

'What will?'

'Smiling.'

'So I'm not the only one who resorts to sarcasm.'

'You're actually admitting it!' she said with a teasing laugh.

'I'm admitting nothing,' he said with another smile, and Candace thought if they kept this up the atmosphere was going to be positively giggly.

'I live in a flat owned by the hospital. It's a stone's throw from Montrose, actually in the grounds but on the far side. There's a block of twelve and they're usually let to visiting doctors, but. . .'

'Because you're a poor little orphan they've let you have one,' she finished for him softly.

He turned his head and eyed her consideringly.

'Something like that. . .yes, but not because I'm an orphan. . .because I'm single, and they're only one-bedroom flats.'

'You'll have to give me directions when we get to the hospital,' she said, 'as I'm only familiar with the College Lawns area and the main hospital complex.'

'Sure thing,' he said lazily, and left her to get on with her driving.

When they stopped in front of a very basic looking apartment block Zac said, 'Welcome to Cell Block H.'

It was a far cry from College Lawns and Candace

didn't doubt that any moment he would point out the fact, but it seemed his mind was in a different channel.

'Care for a coffee?' he asked casually.

He had asked her that once before. Did he remember? she wondered. It hadn't been a pleasant incident for either of them, but it had been before the truce, before she'd realised how he could make her heart leap and her bones melt with longing.

'Yes, that would be nice,' she said with equal airiness.

If the outside of the building was rather bleak, it was not so in Zac's flat, and as she looked around her Candace was amazed at the bright cheerfulness of it. Obviously a man's place but far from austere, with a cream leather suite, mahogany dining table and chairs, bookcases in the same glowing wood, and on the polished floors bright rugs. There were lamps on the windowsills and colourful prints on the walls, and all taken together they made a charming room.

'What an attractive place you've got, Zac,' she exclaimed, and as he raised a dubious eyebrow, 'It is! It's lovely. It makes me think you're not as controlled as you make out if you like light and colour to this extent.'

'I *do* love colour,' he admitted. 'I love brightness and beauty. I suppose it comes of being institutionalised. If I never see grey or cream gloss paint again it won't break my heart.' His voice deepened. '*You're* beautiful, Candace, and until recently I thought that was all you were.'

'And now?'

He was breathing more quickly.

'I'm trying to make up my mind.'

'How very patronising of you!' she flared.

Ignoring her anger, he said, 'Did you know that the

Bible tells us that there was once a queen of Ethiopia called Candace, and the eunuch who was in charge of all her treasures was converted by one of the disciples.'

'No, I didn't,' she breathed.

'It doesn't tell us if she was beautiful, but I think she must have been with such a name.'

'But you call *me* Candy, and I hate it,' she said shakily.

'Maybe it's because I don't want to admit you're different. I don't want to be tempted. It's happened too often that the things I want are out of reach.'

'And you think *I'm* out of reach?' she questioned softly.

'I *know* you are, poor little rich nurse, Uncle Harry's precious niece playing at nursing.'

Pain made her lash out.

'You conceited arrogant chauvinist! You've seen me at work. You know I can do the job. You've even said we work well together. What more do you want. . . blood?'

She was picking up her bag, and it was the same as that other time when they'd had coffee. She was blinded with anger and frustration.

'Goodnight, Zac,' she hissed. 'When you're ready to treat me as a normal human being, let me know. Until then, the less we see of each other the better, as far as I'm concerned,' and she slammed out of the flat.

He caught up with her on the pavement and swung her round to face him.

'*You* might have said goodnight, but *I* haven't.'

He bent and kissed her hard on the lips, and the same fire as before kindled between them, and when he released her he said hoarsely, '*You* might be another Queen Candace, but *I'm* no eunuch. . .and so far I'm not converted.'

* * *

Sunday passed for Candace with an assortment of activities: chores, a phone call to her uncle who was in Portugal and a solitary walk along the nearby common, and all the time in the forefront of her mind speculating as to how Zac might be spending *his* day.

He'd said he was going to be busy, but when Kate had questioned him, he'd been cagey about what he had planned, and Candace found herself sighing, for even though she was fuming at his ostrich-like attitude it didn't stop her from thinking about him constantly.

He had parodied the Bible story to describe themselves, and said that he was no eunuch, but he might as well have been if he behaved like this every time he was attracted to a woman, she thought grimly as she walked unseeingly beside the wild flowers and fresh grasses of the common. Yet no sooner had the thought formed in her mind than she knew that Zac wouldn't be given to casual dalliances, or in fact any kind of dalliance, unless it were with a pleasant, homely sort of girl like Kate. He wouldn't need to question *her* motives, or have to ponder on *her* suitability; it was there for all so see. Feeling disgruntled with life in general, she went to bed early and was rewarded with a restless night.

As she passed through the maternity ward on her way to neonatal on Monday morning, Candace was surprised to see that Kerry Maddox had visitors. An uncomfortable-looking middle-aged couple were hovering beside a small suitcase on one side of the bed, and a lanky youth with a shaved head and a gold ear ornament was lolling at the other. It was the first time she had seen anyone visit the girl, but it looked as if they'd turned up in force to take her and little Kyle home. It was a pity they hadn't been there to support her at the birth, but Candace supposed that, if the lad *was* the father, at least he had eventually put in an appearance. So engrossed was she in the scene that she almost collided with Zac as he came striding through the swing doors with a frown on his face and his white coat flapping.

'Good morning, Candace,' he said briskly, with a noticeable emphasis on her name.

'Good morning, Dr Stephens,' she said circumspectly.

He stopped in mid-stride and asked in a low voice, 'And what is that supposed to mean?'

'I thought a more formal approach would please you. . .that it would make me appear less queenly,' she said blandly, and continued on her way, the epitome of slender efficiency with her gleaming braids coiled neatly beneath a stiff white cap.

Kate appeared in the middle of the morning and said to Candace and Lala, 'We had a patient admitted last night with a molar pregnancy which, as we are all aware, is very rare. *I've* dealt with one in the past, and I think it would be good experience if you both were in on this one. Rowland Ashley is at his private clinic today, so Zac's in charge and I don't envy him. It's a very dangerous situation for any mother to be in, and this one is climbing forty and it's her fourth pregnancy. There were all the signs: vaginal bleeding, excessive nausea brought about by the high levels of human chorionic gonadotrophin or HCG as we call it, that the tumour is producing.

'Zac saw her as soon as he came in this morning and requested ultrasound scanning, which has shown it to be a hydatidiform mole situation. The uterus will have to be completely emptied for although the tumour is benign at this stage, it can turn to cancer if left untreated.'

Candace was casting her mind back to the notes she had made on the subject during training.

'It's when the embryo hasn't developed and tissues from the placenta form a tumour, isn't it?'

Kate smiled.

'You have it. We have to learn about these rare conditions and think we'll never need the knowledge, but it just shows that it's never wasted. In countries like ours, an hydatidiform mole averages only one in two thousand pregnancies, and yet here we are with one at Montrose.'

When she and Lala joined Zac in Theatre, the patient, Helen Drummond, a teacher who had been amazed to find herself pregnant again with three teenage children in the house, had been anaesthetised after having had the seriousness of her condition carefully explained to her. She had been apprehensive and tearful, though the tears had been mainly grief, as she'd just adjusted to the idea of the pregnancy only to be told that there wasn't one in the normal sense of the word.

Zac nodded briefly as Lala stepped in as scrub nurse and Candace placed herself across the operating table from him.

'This is a molar pregnancy,' he said crisply, 'and we have no choice but to induce an abortion to empty the uterus. There is no foetus there, only a tumour consisting of a mass of transparent cysts which you will see closely resemble grapes. It is filling the uterus and must be suctioned out. It's a rare condition that I've only encountered a couple of times.'

Candace nodded, absorbed in what was about to take place, and as the hydatidiform mole came away it was as he'd said—a grapelike formation.

As they scrubbed up afterwards he said, 'This kind

of thing is a sorrow for the patient, but a very necessary exercise, as a chorion carcinoma can develop if the mole is not removed, and Mrs Drummond will be told she must avoid any further pregnancies for at least a year.'

Candace thought that, for all the uncomplicated pregnancies, there was always the one like this, life-threatening, calling for the obstetrician's skill, and she knew that whatever eruptions there might be between Zac and herself outside of health care, there could only ever by respect and admiration on her part when she saw him at work.

Gordon Grampion's voice coming over from the doorway broke into her thoughts, and when she heard what he was saying she immediately tuned in.

'I say, *you* were on strange ground yesterday, Zac,' he said with a sly smile.

He swung round and eyed him coolly.

'I'm not with you, Gordon.'

'Derbyshire. I'd taken a lady-friend for a drive in the countryside, and who should I see but *you* of all people coming out of a desirable residence on the outskirts of one of the rural paradises, and having got a glimpse of the curvy brunette who was waving you off I'd say it looked like time well spent.'

Candace could almost feel Zac withdrawing into himself, but his voice was casual as he said, 'Yes, it was. She's a very attractive girl.'

She flinched. So much for the Zac who wasn't a womaniser, she thought as Gordon ambled off with a knowing wink. So *that* had been his heavy day, then—visiting a woman friend. She sighed. There were different kinds of heaviness, and she wasn't going to start thinking about *that*. . .but what about Kate? They'd seemed very close. . .and then there was herself, and remembering his kiss of Saturday night she found her blood warming and knew she should have more sense. *She* was the last person he was going to fall in love with. He'd had her labelled from the first moment of their meeting, and her mind went back down the years to that night of the hospital dinner dance. She had worn the amber silk dress that still hung in her wardrobe. Other clothes had been cast out, but not that. There were too many memories woven into it.

The vision of Zac across the room, watching her with those dark thoughtful eyes, drawing her to him like a magnet, and the horrifying moment of Camilla's collapse that had been the start of the nightmare, and to some extent the reason for her own presence at Montrose. It had been a disastrous night all round, and so far nothing had given her cause to think otherwise.

Anyone else might have explained that it was a relative, mother or sister that Gordon had seen him with, but not so in Zac's case as he had no family, and she thought wistfully that who was *she* to begrudge him a loving relationship?

She glanced at him quickly, but he was discarding his theatre greens, his face turned away from her. It was clear he wasn't going to offer any explanations to *her*.

Zac came into the labour ward in the early afternoon in response to a call from Kate that he should examine a baby girl that Candace and Lala had delivered seconds earlier. The West Indian nurse had been called away to another imminent birth at the moment the baby arrived and so Candace had been left to check the state of the infant by herself.

She had seen immediately that there were signs of respiratory distress syndrome and sent for Kate, who in turn had put out a call for Zac, and while she was

doing so Candace was putting into practice what she
had learned in training.

There was an increased heartbeat, excessive mucus,
and cyanosis. Remembering how many times she had
been told that the first few minutes of a child's life were
the most vital, she lost no time in trying to persuade
the baby to breathe, with a gentle rubbing of the back,
flicking the soles of the feet, and a few seconds' careful
suctioning with a bulb syringe to clear the airway of
mucus, and thereby lessening the possibility of brain
damage.

Kate was watching in a supervisory capacity, and, to
Candace's relief and delight, by the time Zac appeared,
the baby was breathing normally and the frantic mother
calming down.

He examined it carefully, noting that its heart-rate
and colour had immediately improved, and when the
Apgar score was above six he nodded in satisfaction.

'You seem to have done the trick with this one,
Kate,' he said, 'but obviously you'll need to keep an
eye on her,' and with a brief smile he departed.

Candace watched him go and wondered why the
congratulations were for Kate instead of herself. *She'd*
been the one to raise the alarm and start the treatment.
Maybe he thought she might get too big for her boots
if he threw her too many crumbs, she thought wryly,
and wondered if the dark-haired beauty Gordon had
been so impressed with had the standard of excellence
that Zachary Stephens called for in every aspect of life.

As the weeks went by, Candace became increasingly
aware that, although she and Zac were of necessity
frequently in each other's company jobwise, he was
barely on the perimeter of her social life, if she could
claim to have one.

She had been to the cinema a couple of times with Lala, had seen a show at the local theatre on her own, and had spent a couple of weekends at the house in Belgravia with the intention of looking up some acquaintances, only to change her mind each time she got there, and she had ended up reading, watching TV and making lukewarm forays around the stores.

Her uncle was still in Portugal. He'd bought a villa just outside Faro and was contemplating retiring there, and in spite of his affectionate assurances that nothing need change, and he would love to have her there with him, she felt isolated and alone.

The job was the only thing that brought any comfort, and as the days went by on the maternity unit she often asked herself how she'd endured the boredom of her previous existence. But, of course, in those days she hadn't been bored. She had thought that living in the lap of luxury was great, and it wasn't until she had lost Camilla and met Zachary Stephens that she had realised there was more to life than being forever on the carousel.

She presumed that Zac was still spending his Sundays in Derbyshire, for whenever Gordon quizzed him about it he never made any attempt to deny it, and she had noticed that he was always very preoccupied on Monday mornings.

It was on a Monday, which for some reason was always the most traumatic day of the week, that they crossed the barrier between their public and private lives again.

Candace had succumbed to a mini-virus over the weekend which had caused her to feel dreadful on the Saturday, somewhat better on Sunday, and almost back to normal on Monday morning, but the vomiting and other effects of it had left her feeling drained and listless, and as she presented herself at Montrose she knew that she needed another day to throw it off completely.

The trouble was that Kate wasn't around, the labour ward was full, and when Lala and Debbie arrived the pleasant dark-skinned nurse had a badly sprained wrist, and Debbie was on edge because her little boy had been sick on the way to school and she was half expecting a phone call to say she must come and get him.

Zac was already there looking somewhat frayed himself, and as the night staff were going off duty one of them whispered, 'I think our friend Zachary got out of the wrong side of the bed this morning, and as he looks somewhat jaded we've been wondering whose bed he got out of. I wouldn't mind it being mine if it weren't for the fact that my Bob would object.'

He was eyeing Candace sourly.

'When you've finished gossiping, perhaps you'd like to assist me?'

She flushed. It was the other girl who'd been gossiping. *She* hadn't spoken a word. No doubt he would be even more liverish if he knew that *he'd* been the subject of her remarks.

'Yes, of course,' she said equably, determined that he wasn't going to make her feel any worse than she did already, but her pleasantness didn't seem to be taking the edge off his irritation. He was frowning, and as she eyed him warily he said, 'I've had one hell of a night. I only got back from Derbyshire at seven o'clock this morning and was called out immediately as Rowland has gone to pick up young Henry from boarding school. . .and as usual Gordon couldn't be found. So if I'm not at my best, it's because I've got an empty stomach and a. . .'

'Failing libido?' she questioned sweetly.

'I was about to say a severe headache, if you must know,' he snapped. 'It's damned cold out in the open even on a summer night.'

Candace stared at him. What was that supposed to mean? That he and his brown-haired lady friend had spent the night under the stars?

'Yes, well, I suppose it's whatever turns you on, but I must say that lying in the gorse doesn't seem to have improved your personality. I'd say that you and the bush are about as prickly as each other.'

He was eyeing her thoughtfully.

'You can be very obtuse at times, Candace. You stand there looking like something out of *Vogue*, pontificating about things you know nothing about.'

She picked him up on the first part of the sentence.

'*Vogue*! In an NHS uniform, and feeling ghastly.'

'What do you mean?' he asked, dark eyes raking her face.

'I've been ill over the weekend, that's all, and am not as fit as I thought I'd be today.'

'And you were alone?'

'Well, yes, of course. How else would I be?'

'You should have rung me.'

'Where at. . .Derbyshire? How would I have known where to find you? And I'm sure you would have liked that. . .my interrupting your moorland idyll.'

He smiled, but his eyes were still sombre as he said, 'You're doing it again. . .jumping to conclusions.'

She *had* to ask. 'In what way?'

'Assuming that I wouldn't have wanted to know you were ill.'

Her heart began to sing. Maybe he *did* care, but his next words showed in what context.

'After all, I *am* a doctor, and that being so I'm

ordering you to go home. Kate wouldn't want you here if you're not fit.'

'I'm staying,' she said flatly. 'I'm over the worst, and the other two girls have got problems of their own this morning.'

CHAPTER FIVE

DURING the day Candace found herself flagging; everything was an effort and she couldn't wait to get home and slump into bed. The actual virus had gone, but she would never have believed it could have left her feeling so jaded, and if Kate had been there instead of having taken a day's leave to accompany the bereaved husband to his son's school, she would have obeyed Zac's instructions and gone off sick.

When she let herself into the apartment, it was cool and very quiet and she sighed with relief. Now she could unwind, feel sorry for herself in private, and after a bath she was going to bed.

When the doorbell rang, she gave an exasperated groan. She was in no mood for visitors, or door-to-door salespeople, or suchlike.

Zac was standing on the doorstep and as he eyed her wan face he said, 'I was hoping to catch you before you left, but I wasn't quick enough. Every time I've seen you today, you've looked far from well and I've been visualising you coming home to an empty apartment, missing your evening meal, and going straight to bed.'

Candace tried to manage a smile.

'Right on every count,' she told him. 'That was exactly what I had in mind.'

'Fair enough,' he agreed, 'but if you could bring yourself to invite me in, I'll tell you what *I* have in mind,' and as she stepped back to let him pass he said, 'I've brought some fish.'

'Fish!' she echoed. 'What sort? What for?'

76

'Cod, in answer to the first question, to make us a meal is the answer to the second, and *then* you can go to bed. When last did you eat?'

'Saturday, some time,' she said vaguely.

He tutted irritably.

'It's no wonder you feel ill! Nobody fires on all cylinders without food inside them.'

'I don't think I could eat anything,' she said faintly, as she tried to adjust to the fact that Zac was in her apartment with a parcel of wet fish, a bag of new potatoes, and a choice cauliflower.

He followed her glance and said with a tight smile, 'It won't be anything spectacular, just basic cooking, but as long as you're not continuing to feel nauseous it should do you a world of good.'

Candace pointed to the kitchen wordlessly, and as Zac placed the food on the worktop he said, 'Give me forty-five minutes,' and she thought that if he was as efficient in the kitchen as he was in Theatre it might be worth waiting for.

'I'll go and have a bath, then,' she said in the same amazed voice.

'Do that,' he agreed crisply, and, taking a plastic apron off a hook by the door, he began to prepare the food, and she was dismissed.

The long hot soak would normally have washed away her tensions, but the thought of Zac busying himself in her kitchen was hardly conducive to relaxation, and so when she presented herself in the doorway wrapped in a pink towelling robe, with her hair hanging limply around her pale face, there was no miraculous transformation for him to see.

'I'll bet I look a far cry from *Vogue* at *this* moment,' she said drily as she heaved herself up on to a kitchen stool.

He was stirring some kind of sauce, and at her words he took his eyes off the pan for a second and said with an amused sort of relish, 'Yes, you do. In fact you look a mess, but we'll soon have you fighting fit again. A meal and a good night's sleep will work wonders.'

There were other things that would work wonders, too, she thought wretchedly, like taking her in his arms and soothing away the mental pain for which there was never any cure, caused by the misery of loving a prickly customer like himself, who seemed to have plenty of irons in the fire but none of them heated for her.

They ate at the kitchen table, hardly the most romantic of settings, with Zac in an old sweater and jeans, and Candace hunched in the robe, her tangled hair still flat against her head, and dark shadows beneath her eyes. A bottle of orange squash was the first thing he had laid hands on in the fridge, vintage unknown, and the rays of the evening sun made up for the lack of candles.

So far they had shared two disastrous coffee breaks and now they'd moved up one, they were actually sharing a meal, but once again the ambience was in short supply, and this time *she* was mostly to blame.

When Zac placed the food in front of her, Candace realised that she *was* hungry, and the cod in mustard sauce with the crisp vegetables was delicious. He hadn't been able to resist a dig, however.

'I know that you're probably accustomed to turbot or brill or suchlike, but at five-thirty in the evening the fishmonger hasn't much to offer.'

To her everlasting shame Candace felt tears prick her eyes. Why did he have to keep doing this? If the trappings of her life were different from his, what did it matter? It was what they were inside that counted.

Zac had seen the tears, and was on his feet, moving

around the table. He put his arm around her shoulders
and said softly, 'I'm sorry. I don't know why I say
things like that to you. I don't behave like that with
anyone else.' His voice deepened. 'It's not envy, you
know, Candace. In fact, I don't know what the hell it
is.'

So he was admitting that he only treated her like
this, she thought wretchedly, and unable to force it
back, she gave a gulping sob.

'Don't,' he said hoarsely. 'Please don't cry. God! I
should be kicked. You're not well, and I'm making you
feel even worse.'

'It's all right, Zac,' she whispered, pulling away from
him. 'I know I irritate you for some reason, and I've
long since given up trying to fathom why. Let's finish
the meal, shall we?'

He went back to his own side of the table.

'Yes, of course. I shouldn't be insisting you have
nourishment and then putting you off your food.'

She gave him a watery smile.

'It was good of you to take the trouble.'

'Don't mention it. I can't let Kate's staff fade away
from illness and malnutrition in her absence,' he said
lightly.

'Oh, I see. This is all on Kate's account,' she said,
feeling the tears rise again.

'What do you *think*, Candace?' he asked, as gravity
replaced the flippancy.

She pushed the plate away.

'I'm blessed if I know, Zac.' And, getting to her
feet, she said, 'But thanks anyway, and now I'm going
to bed. Lock up as you go out, will you?'

When Candace opened her eyes the next morning she
sensed immediately that she wasn't alone in the apart-

ment. She had lived a solitary existence long enough to know the difference, and instinct warned her of another presence. Surely Zac had locked up securely when he'd left? she thought uneasily, but as she tiptoed out of the bedroom the sense of someone else in the place was overwhelming.

He was taking toast from under the grill, coffee was percolating nearby, and from the state of his clothes it looked as if he had slept in them.

As Candace gazed at him in sleepy amazement, Zac said briskly, 'And how are *you* this morning?'

'Er. . .much better,' she told him faintly. 'But what are *you* doing here? Didn't you go home?'

'No. I had some notes to write up, and thought I'd do them here so that I could keep an eye on you, and then it got late and. . .'

'Where did you sleep?' she asked in continuing amazement.

'In one of your comfy chairs, when I wasn't checking up on you, and apart from a crick in my neck I feel fine.'

'You mean you've been watching me while I was asleep?' she questioned weakly.

His eyes didn't meet hers as he replied flippantly, 'Yes, I do it all the time. I'm a doctor, remember? And I can assure you that you don't snore or sleep with your mouth open; in fact you do it beautifully.'

Candace eyed him balefully. Would they ever have a normal conversation? He was buttering the toast and, pointing to its golden crispness, he said, 'If you're intending reporting for duty at the mighty Montrose this morning, you've just got time for toast and coffee. I've had mine, and now I'm going home to change.'

His eyes were on her smooth shoulders above the silk nightgown and the swell of her firm breasts inside it, and Candace eyed him back challengingly. Zac disapproved of her allure, her background, the fact that she'd showed up on his patch. The only thing they had in common was a sexual sort of chemistry, and it wasn't enough. It might have been for the Candace of the old days, but not now. She didn't want him lusting after her without love, without respect, and so she ignored the treacherous warming of her blood and said coolly, 'Toast and coffee will be fine, and you really didn't have to concern yourself about me. I can cope.'

His face closed up. He'd got the message.

'Yes, I can see you can, and that being so, I'll be off.'

Candace was biting into a piece of toast, for all the world as if it were a normal occurrence to be breakfasting with Zachary Stephens. The only difference was that most couples who breakfasted together had slept together, and she had no intentions of giving her body to a man who was enmeshed with one woman and extremely friendly with another.

'Sure, I'll see you at Montrose, then, Zac,' she said, swinging a long bare leg as she stirred her coffee, and with a baffled nod he picked up a sheaf of papers and departed.

'Zac tells me that you're not well,' Kate said when they met on the wards that morning. Candace smiled.

'Past tense. I picked up a bug over the weekend and thought I'd thrown it off, but yesterday I felt quite rough. However, I'm fine this morning after a good night's sleep.'

'Good,' Kate replied, 'as Debbie's little boy isn't well, so we're going to be one short today.'

'Did you have a nice day yesterday?' Candace asked.

Kate's homely face softened.

'You mean with Rowland and young Henry? Yes.
He's a cute young kid and should be at home instead
of at boarding school. I keep telling his father that he
needs a stable home life now, more than ever, instead
of being packed off there. His mother's sister would
help, I know, and Rowland knows that *I'll* do anything
I can to assist.'

She gave an embarrassed laugh. 'Why is it that we
women folk are so uncomplicated and the men so much
the opposite? There's Rowland, all tied up in suffering
knots over a woman who didn't deserve him, Gordon,
who's only motivated by the sight of a pair of nice legs,
and Zac, darling Zac, who's worth more than all the
male staff put together, tough as they come, handsome
enough to make any woman's heart beat faster, and
yet so uptight sometimes.'

Don't I know it? Candace thought, and then, as the
memory of him serving up the meal that he had taken
the trouble to prepare for her nudged her conscience,
she admitted to herself that there *was* a soft core inside
him. She had seen it in his treatment of his mothers
and babies, in the respect he showed Kate, and last
night, unbelievably, *she'd* been shown a glimpse of it.

The day that Candace and Zac had started together
in her kitchen proved to be a sad one for the unit. A
girl had been brought in off the streets in the last stages
of pregnancy; dirty and dishevelled, she'd been sleeping rough, and though she was somewhat incoherent
they had been able to establish that she'd received no
pre-natal care whatsoever.

A passer-by had seen her staggering along the pavement clutching at her distended stomach, and groping
around as if she couldn't see, and had sent for an
ambulance.

By the time the girl had been admitted to Montrose

she was experiencing breathing difficulties and kept having convulsions, during which her body jerked in violent rhythmic movements.

'Ugh! She's filthy!' one of the nurses in Reception said as they laid her on the bed, and Zac had glared at her.

'She's also in a very serious condition,' he had snapped as he examined her. 'The kid's got eclampsia by the looks of it, and there isn't going to be time for shampoos and showers. Wipe her down with some sterile cloths for the time being. I'm going to insert an endotracheal tube and inject an anticonvulsive drug, and then I'm going to organise a speedy Caesarean section, hoping that we'll be in time. I'd guess that the girl will have had pre-eclampsia for some time, and as she's had no care it will have gone unrecognised until this very serious situation developed.'

Candace had listened in dismay. It was a bad case of toxaemia, and she was so very young. . .and so very sick. What was she doing among the homeless? The few words she had uttered had been in an educated voice, and her filthy clothes had been of good quality when they were new, but somewhere along the way she had come adrift, and her blighted young life had been made worse by an unwanted pregnancy, for who in their right mind would consider having a child in those conditions?

On the few occasions that the girl opened her eyes there had been a blankness in them, and when they had tried to get her to tell them her name she'd mumbled, 'Haven't got one.'

Candace had seen Zac perform before and his dedication was without question, but when the foetus was born lifeless, and didn't respond to any of his frantic measures, she had the opportunity to see the true depth of his caring. His face was white, his dark eyes almost black with the emotions he was holding in check, and she wanted to take him into her arms and comfort him, but the trauma wasn't over.

The girl's eyes opened for a second. They were wide, blue, and questioning, in a moment's lucidity. They all knew she had to have an answer, and when he shook his head slowly, she gave a tired little sigh and closed them again. Candace saw that her lips were turning blue, her bony young chest had stopped lifting and falling with each shallow breath, and she knew they had been too late. Lack of care and nourishment had played their part, and in spite of their efforts at resuscitation it was as if once having slipped out of their reach she had no desire to come back.

Candace found Zac in his office, and when she went in he was standing by the window, his shoulders hunched as if against a chill wind.

'Zac,' she said softly.

He turned round slowly.

'What?' he rasped.

'Don't be like this,' she pleaded. 'You *have* to be impersonal about these kind of happenings or you would never cope; none of us would.'

His eyes were weary.

'I know that, Candace. There's no need to remind me, but what a waste of two young lives. If only we could have drawn her into our circle of care, or if only she'd had the sense to take precautions.'

'If two of them are huddled inside a cardboard box for warmth and they find comfort from each other's bodies, it's hardly likely that there'll be a condom or a packet of the Pill to hand,' she said quietly, 'not when the effort to merely survive is so great.

'There was no fault here with you, Zac,' she went

on, 'nor with Montrose. The fault lies within the system.'

He nodded grimly.

'As it did with me.'

'Yes, in a way,' she agreed, and then because she had thought it more than once, and wondered what the answer would be, in spite of it being hardly the right moment, she asked, 'Have you ever tried to trace your parents?'

His face was bleak.

'You mean the original tear-jerker? Abandoned child's search for parents? No. Never. And I never will. Why should I? It wouldn't blot out all the misery. I was left to a life of loneliness that I never asked for. I've come through it and am content. It's a contentment that was hard-won, and nothing that lies in my past is going to shatter it.'

Candace walked across and touched his cheek gently.

'I hope that nothing that lies in your future will shatter it either,' she said softly, and as he surveyed her with surprised eyes she left him and went back to her duties.

Late on Friday afternoon of the same week, Candace received a message to say that someone was waiting to see her in the hospital foyer, and when she got there she was amazed to find Roddy Carstairs.

It was years since she had seen him. The last time had been a few weeks after Camilla's death, when she had been so traumatised that he'd been uneasy in her company and had beat a speedy retreat. After that, he'd steered clear of her, though it had barely registered, and now here he was at Montrose.

As she eyed him in surprise, Candace saw that the lanky, effeminate youth of over four years ago was now a maturer, heftier man, but as they shook hands she saw that he still had the languid, affected manner that had irritated her then.

'This *is* a surprise, Roddy,' she said pleasantly. 'How did you know I was here?'

'Your uncle mentioned it. I visited him as I was passing through Portugal a couple of weeks ago, and he said you were here.' He was eyeing her admiringly. 'It suits you, Candace.'

'What does?'

'The uniform. It's hardly Bond Street, but it suits you.'

She frowned.

'I'm sure you've not come north just to tell me that.'

'No, of course not. I'm in the area on business. I've joined the family firm, thought I'd better show willing. I decided to look you up.'

'Why now?' she asked. 'We've not seen each other for years.'

He smiled, and Candace thought that he was certainly an improvement on the old Roddy.

'I've been busy getting married. . .and divorced.'

'Really? I wasn't aware that you were involved in either state of bliss.'

He was laughing now, a booming sound that made heads turn.

'The words of a true cynic.'

It was her turn to laugh.

'Not really. I've no experience of either situation.'

His eyes glinted.

'Good! Perhaps we can get together, then. You're just as stunning as ever, Candace.'

'Am I?' she said drily. 'Well, just remember there is more than one meaning to the word.'

'I'm in town for a couple of nights,' he said, ignoring the warning. 'Can I take you out to dinner?'

Candace hesitated. He might be an improvement on his old self, but did she want to spend the evening with him? The answer to that was no, and she was just about to tell him so when Zac came striding through in his outdoor clothes and carrying a holdall. Rowland Ashley was with him and Zac was smiling at something the older man had said. When he saw her with Roddy his face straightened and his eyes held a question, but he didn't stop, just gave her a casual wave and went on his way, calling over his shoulder, 'Remember, Rowland, I'm only in the next county if you need me.'

Her spirits dropped. So now it wasn't just Sundays. He was going to the country for the whole weekend. That made her own break seem empty and pointless.

'Yes, all right, Roddy,' she said. 'Where shall I meet you?'

'I'll pick you up,' he offered.

'No. I'll meet you in town,' she insisted, knowing that she didn't want him to come to the apartment.

'All right,' he agreed. 'Just say the place and I'll be there.'

Roddy hadn't forgotten that she had expensive tastes. He had booked a table at the town's most exclusive restaurant, and as they were being seated Candace's mind went back to the meal she'd shared with Zac earlier in the week. There could be no comparison between the two. Whatever this place had to offer, champagne, caviar, oysters, it wouldn't be as enjoyable as Zac's cod in mustard sauce, because he had taken the trouble to make it for her. He'd shopped for the food and cooked it, and how she wished it had been because he craved her company, instead of an act of concern for a sick member of staff.

As they ate the luxurious meal, Roddy was eyeing her consideringly and eventually he said, 'Meeting you again, it seems incredible that you're not married and having to rush off and make a meal for some guy, although, thinking back to the old days, it would be a case of *him* making a meal for *you*, eh, Candace?'

She smiled.

'So you're surprised I'm not married, Roddy? Well, as we both know, life *is* full of surprises.'

She wasn't going to tell this rather pompous upper class acquaintance from time back that she'd been sidetracked from the usual progression of love, court-ship, and marriage by grief, a new way of life, and meeting a very attractive and unusual man, who by now would be out among the Derbyshire dales, spending the weekend with some other woman.

When he saw that she wasn't going to explain the reason for her single state Roddy started to chat about London and people they both knew, and how much he was having to pay his ex-wife.

'So who did you marry, Roddy?' she asked, only mildly curious.

'Belinda Smart. Her father's a banker.'

'And what went wrong?'

'We got married because she was pregnant, but she had a miscarriage, which made it all seem a bit pointless.'

Candace stared at him.

'So you didn't love each other?'

'No,' he said easily. 'Only slept with her once and bingo, she was pregnant. She was scared of an abortion, so we decided to make it legal.'

'It hardly sounds a firm basis for marriage,' she commented drily, imagining Zac's anger if he'd heard Roddy's flippant attitude to procreation.

'Yes, well, as I said, the divorce has just come

through.' His eyes gleamed. 'Which means I'm free again.'

'Yes, so you are,' she agreed, 'but don't come looking at me. I'm quite happy as I am.' It wasn't strictly true, but it certainly applied as far as *he* was concerned.

'Yes, but you could be happier. There are varying degrees of it, you know,' he said smoothly.

She didn't need to be told that, and it was on the tip of her tongue to tell him that she'd rather have five minutes' misery with a certain Zachary Stephens than a lifetime of *his* interpretation of it, but she didn't have to hold back the words because what he was saying now had her riveted.

'Talking about wedded bliss or the lack of it, what about your uncle? Is he thinking of tying the knot after all these years?'

Candace blinked. Had she heard aright?

'What do you mean?'

'Told you I visited him at his place in Portugal, didn't I?'

'Yes, and. . .?' she asked impatiently.

'There was a very attractive widow staying there, and it was easy to see they were very close. Hasn't he told you?'

'Why should he?' she said lightly, concealing her amazement. 'Uncle Harry's life is his own business.'

'So you're not surprised?'

She was dumbfounded. Was the only safe and secure part of her life going to change now? Her uncle was the rock that she had clung to when her parents were killed, and his loving kindness had been just as unswerving when it was Camilla's turn to leave her. She would never begrudge him happiness, but why now, at coming up to sixty years old, should he decide

to break the habits of a lifetime? It was most probably
Roddy putting two and two together and getting the
wrong answer, she told herself, as she said coolly, 'No,
why should I be?' and glancing at her watch, 'I have to
be up early in the morning, I've a busy day ahead of
me. I'm afraid I'm going to have to go, Roddy. Thank
you for a delightful meal.'

His face tightened.

'So you're not going to invite me back for a nightcap?
You used to in the old days.'

She gave him a conciliatory smile.

'With the life I lead, and the hours I keep, the only
nightcap that would be on offer is one with a bobble
on it.' And on that note she gathered up her things,
got to her feet, and strolled out of the restaurant,
leaving him to follow.

By the time that Roddy had paid for the meal and
caught up with her, Candace was standing beneath the
restaurant's striped awning, car keys dangling from her
fingers. The urge to be gone was evident in every line
of her.

'Surely you're not in such a rush,' he said huffily.

'It's Saturday tomorrow,' she said obtusely.

'So? You don't work Saturdays, do you?'

'Er—no, but it's always a busy day none the less.'

'You won't come out with me tomorrow, then?
Before I go back to London?'

'I don't think so,' she said with a half-hearted show
of regret, 'but if you're this way again we could. . .'

That perked him up, and he proceeded to dismay
her by saying, 'I'll be up here once a week for the next
couple of months. It will be just an overnight stay, but
I'll certainly take you up on the offer.'

'Yes, do,' she agreed faintly, and knew she had only
herself to blame.

By the time Candace got back to the apartment, her amazed hurt regarding Roddy's comments about her uncle was subsiding. She kept telling herself firmly that if he *was* planning anything so surprising *she* would be the first to know, but it didn't stop her having a restless night, during which she dreamt that he and Zac were having a double wedding, while *she* was being pursued down a long winding road by Roddy. The faces of both brides were in shadow, and no matter how she tried she couldn't distinguish them.

On Saturday afternoon, while strolling around the busy open-air market, Candace met Kate and her mother, and the three of them ended up having coffee at one of the pavement cafés beside the stalls. They chatted about various things, and then, unable to help herself, Candace said casually, 'I saw Zac dashing off yesterday. I presume he's away for the weekend?'

Kate's face became solemn, and, watching her, Candace couldn't tell if there was anxiety or annoyance in her eyes as she said, 'Yes, he's gone to Derbyshire again. His involvement there seems to be the thing uppermost in his mind these days. It is a total commitment that he's considering. I just hope he's thought it through, and knows what he's doing.'

'Me too,' Candace said gravely, unable to face any further probing, and wishing she knew exactly what was going on. It seemed as if Kate *did* have feelings for him, and that made two of them, and a third who could command his full attention from the sound of it.

As she let herself back into the apartment the words were ringing in her head like a death knell to her hopes. 'Total commitment'. It usually meant only one thing, a one-to-one relationship, and the thought of it made her feel physically sick. Yet she knew she had no cause to be. Zac had never made any advances to her.

She was the one who had kissed *him* in the gardens that day, and thinking back to the Candace of time past she knew that *she* would have let him know she wanted him, as having what she wanted had been part of her pampered lifestyle. Whereas the girl who looked back at her from her bedroom mirror had learned to her cost that everything was not there for the taking.

Candace phoned her uncle in the early evening. They always spoke at least once each week, and this time she was more eager than usual to hear his voice.

When a woman's soft tones came over the line at the villa in Monte Gordo, Candace tensed, and then immediately told herself that Uncle Harry didn't live like a monk. He often had friends of both sexes in his house.

'Hold on a moment, my dear,' she said. 'I'll get him for you,' and within seconds his deep, familiar voice was speaking into her ear.

'Candace! How are you?'

'I'm fine, Uncle Harry,' she said. 'How are you?'

'On top of the world,' he said with a happy chuckle.

'Good,' and then because she *had* to know, 'You'll never guess who showed up at the hospital yesterday.'

'No, I don't suppose I will,' he said fondly. 'Who was it?'

'Someone who's visited you recently at your Portuguese retreat.'

There was silence for a moment, and then he said cautiously, 'Carstairs? Young Roddy?'

'Yes.'

'Ah, I see, and he told you I wasn't alone?'

'He always was a gossip,' she said lightly.

Candace could imagine Harry's craggy face sobering and the kind blue eyes anxious at the conversation that was taking place between them.

'Listen, love,' he said slowly. 'I'm mortified that an outsider should get to you first with what is going on here. I haven't told you before because I wanted to make sure the lady would have me. I only popped the question this afternoon, and when she said yes, my first thought was to tell *you* that I'm getting married. I phoned but you weren't in, and I decided to leave it until later. Be happy for me, Candace,' he said.

She took a deep breath.

'I *am* happy for you,' she told him sincerely. 'Your own joy is there in your voice and in what you're saying to me, but who is the lucky lady?'

'Margot Garcia is her name,' he said softly. 'I knew her a long time ago, but was so obsessed with making money that I let true happiness escape me. *She* came to Portugal and married a business rival of mine, and has lived in Faro ever since. She is the reason I bought this place. Now that I've found her again I can't bear to let her out of my sight.'

'It all sounds very romantic, Uncle Harry,' she said gently. 'I'd love to meet her.'

'You will, my dear. There's going to be a wedding very soon, and I won't allow it to take place without my beautiful niece being present. You'll come to Monte Gordo for me, won't you, Candace?'

She laughed.

'Just try stopping me. I'll need a little warning so that I can arrange leave from Montrose, but nothing will keep me away, believe me.'

CHAPTER SIX

ZAC had come back from Derbyshire in enigmatic mood, and when they met on the wards on Monday morning Candace eyed him thoughtfully. When she asked if he'd had a nice weekend he looked at her blankly for a moment and then said urbanely, 'Yes, it was very meaningful.'

She didn't know what that was supposed to mean and wasn't going to ask, but the phrase had the same depressing sound to it as 'total commitment'. It seemed that *he* had a question for *her*.

'Who was the guy hovering over you in Reception on Friday afternoon?'

'Someone I used to know in my idle youth,' she said with a smile.

He returned the smile, but there was a barb in his reply.

'So you still haven't outgrown all that?'

'All what?' she asked warily.

'The glitzy ritzy stuff.'

'I haven't seen Roddy in years,' she protested angrily, 'and if you can't tell that I've changed there's no point in my answering the question, but while you're analysing me, why not take a look at yourself? If ever there was a case of harking back to one's origins. . . you're it!'

To her surprise he began to laugh, and her annoyance increased as he said mildly, 'Yes, I suppose it *would* take surgery to remove the chip off my shoulder, unless you know of any natural cures?'

94

She gave him a long hard look and went on her way, thinking that there was the most natural cure in the world available, that would take away both their nightmares, but it only worked if taken together, and Zac was finding *his* solace elsewhere.

A patient of Rowland Ashley's, who had been in the unit for some weeks, had started in premature labour, and there was a mixture of excitement and concern among the staff.

Janet McCready was thirty-three years old, a quiet, pleasant woman married to an architect. Her hopes of motherhood would have never materialised if she hadn't had fertility tests which had resulted in her being given the drug clomiphene along with gonadotrophin hormone, and now to the couple's great joy, she was expecting triplets.

Rowland had been sent for, and in the meantime Zac had decided that it was excessive stretching of the uterus that had stimulated contractions that in turn had led to premature labour.

It had been arranged for Janet to have a Caesarean section in ten days' time, but nature had decreed otherwise.

'I could give her salbutamol or turbutaline to attempt to halt the labour,' she heard him tell Gordon, 'but I don't know what Rowland would want. He might decide to bring them.'

When the senior obstetrician arrived that *was* his decision, and Candace was disappointed that Kate and the other two obstetrics assistants were to be in attendance, while she was designated to prepare the incubators that the three babies would require.

She liked Janet McCready, admired the stoic calm she had displayed during the long weeks of waiting, and would have loved to be there to see her children born, but if anyone knew that each spoke of the wheel was as important as the rest, she did. When Zac came jubilantly out of Theatre followed by the other two men her heart lifted to see his joy.

'Three girls, Candace,' he said. 'All in a good condition, and a happy, exhausted mother. We've done our bit. It's up to you now.'

'Not entirely, I hope,' she said with a nervous smile.

'No, of course not. The others will be along as soon as they've scrubbed up.'

It was later that day that a dreadful thing occurred. The McCready babies were progressing well in their incubators. One of them, Lillian, had needed artificial ventilation to assist her breathing originally, but was now managing without help, and the others, who appeared to be stronger than she, were giving no cause for concern.

Candace had gone for her break leaving Lala and Debbie in charge of the new arrivals. When she got back, she saw to her surprise that the room was empty, and as she hurried forward to check on their charges she heard a young child's laughter, yet there was no one to be seen, until her glance went to the far side of the incubator at the end and her stomach knotted with horror.

A small boy of not more than two years old had his fist through one of the handholes in the side and was pulling the baby towards him. In the split-second that Candace realised what was happening and flung herself towards the child, Zac's voice bellowed from behind like an enraged bull.

'What the hell is going on, Candace?'

She didn't answer. She was easing the child's grip off the baby's tiny arm and pulling the toddler to one side.

'Come here, Errol!' a shrill voice called from the doorway. 'You shouldn't be in 'ere.' A young mother with frizzed hair, a tight skirt and a black leather jacket came forward and grabbed his hand.

'He most certainly shouldn't!' Candace told her in furious agreement. 'Visitors to this unit are supposed to keep their children under control.'

Chewing on a piece of gum, the girl said cockily, 'All right, no need to get your knickers in a twist. He's only a baby.'

'Not so much of a baby as the one he was trying to drag out of the incubator,' Candace yelled angrily.

The mother marched off at such a fast pace that her child's feet were barely touching the floor, and Candace turned to Zac, who was examining the infant Lillian with a face like thunder.

'Lucky for you, it looks as if no harm's been done,' he gritted. She was about to explain how she had come back and found them unattended but he forestalled her.

'What do you think you're playing at, Candace, letting outsiders in here? You know how important it is to protect the babies from infection. That kid's hands were filthy, and it's a wonder he didn't pull the baby's arm off the way he was tugging. I'd have thought better of you than this, but I should have known.'

'I suppose you mean that you can't make a silk purse out of a sow's ear?' she said tonelessly. 'Once a drone, always a drone.'

There was the sound of hurrying feet and Lala came running in.

'Oh, is everything all right?' she gasped. 'Debbie got a phone call to say that her mother has died, and she

was in such a state of shock, I had to help her through
to Kate's office.'

Zac's face went blank.

'So who was on duty in here, Lala?' he asked grimly.

'Debbie and me. Candace was on her break.' She
looked around her uneasily. 'Why, is something
wrong?'

'A child had wandered in here and was trying to drag
one of the babies out of its incubator,' Candace said
quietly, her face white and drawn.

'Oh, my God!' Lala whispered. 'I'll be hung, drawn
and quartered for this.'

'I don't think so,' Candace told her. 'It's already
been done,' and, turning her back on them both, she
went about her duties, knowing that if Zac followed
her to apologise she would either burst into tears or hit
him.

He didn't. When she turned her head he had gone,
and Lala asked shakenly, 'What did you mean?'

'He'd already torn a strip off *me*. He thought *I* was
to blame.'

Lala's face was creased in dismay.

'I'm sorry, Candace. I really am, but at least he
knows now that it wasn't your fault.'

'Yes, he does,' she agreed slowly, 'but it doesn't
alter the fact that if the wind blew his hat off, he'd
blame *me*.'

The apology came that same evening when Candace
opened her door to find Zac standing on the mat. She
glared at him coldly and made to shut him out, but he
wedged his foot inside and told her with an ironic
smile, 'I used to be a bailiff.'

She wasn't amused.

'And a bigoted, fault-finding jumper to the wrong

conclusions as well?' she said coldly as she stepped back for him to enter.

He shrugged.

'I suppose if the cap fits. . .but I've come to apologise. I'm afraid that I let myself become too intense about some things.'

'Your dislike of me being one of them?'

A shadow came over his face.

'Is that really how you see it, Candace?'

'How else?' she asked coldly. 'I can't put a foot right with you.'

His eyes were dark and fathomless as he said, 'I've told you already that I don't know why you have that effect on me. You're classy, beautiful, and efficient, and I. . .'

'Efficient!' she hooted. 'Since when? You couldn't wait to bawl me out today, could you? I tried to explain, but you were making such a meal of finding fault with me, I couldn't get a word in edgeways.'

He pursed his lips ruefully.

'Was I that bad?'

'You know you were, Zac,' she cried angrily. 'I understood you being so incensed at what had happened, any one of us would have felt the same, but of course you didn't have to look for a scapegoat. I was a sitting duck.'

'Have you finished?' he asked, tight faced.

'No, I haven't. I'm glad you called. It will save me telling you tomorrow. You've won. I'm leaving Montrose. I shall give Kate my notice in the morning. There must be other maternity units in the land where the obstetricians are easier to work with.'

He lowered himself on to her couch and surveyed her with dismayed eyes.

'Don't go, Candace,' he said flatly. 'I couldn't live

with myself if I drove you away. Will you change your mind if I promise to keep out of your way. . .and keep my comments to myself?'

She had told him she was leaving on the spur of the moment. It wasn't a planned announcement, and as soon as she had said it she wanted to bite the words back, and mercifully Zac was offering her a way out.

She made herself pause, and then said with weary slowness, 'I suppose so. After all, why *should* I let you drive me away? I've done nothing wrong. All I want is to be allowed to get on with my life and my career.'

He got to his feet.

'That's fair enough. The least I can do is allow you to do that,' he said gravely, and then he went.

When he had gone, Candace slumped down in the place where he had sat. She could still feel the warmth of him on the cushions and there was comfort in it. Time went by and she continued to sit there, deep in thought, and when she finally stirred herself she had decided that she *was* going to get on with her life, and if it didn't include Zac, too bad.

The week that followed was a strange mixture of peace and misery. The peace came from Zac's promise to steer clear of her, the misery was because now there was nothing between them—no aggro, no rapport, no friendship. . .nothing.

There were the usual emergencies on the unit, but each time Zac turned out to be elsewhere, and for once Gordon Grampion was seen to be earning his keep.

One afternoon in the middle of the week Debbie called Candace over to a patient in labour.

'We've got a prolapsed cord here,' she said seriously, pointing to where both the umbilical cord and the baby were presenting themselves at the entrance to the vagina. The cord was clearly visible and both nurses knew that if it should become trapped between the baby and the mother's bony pelvis, it would cut off the blood supply to the child and it would die. Immediate action was required, in the first instance by placing the patient in a knee to chest position to relieve the pressure on the cord, and in the second by having a doctor assess the problem without delay.

'What's wrong?' the mother-to-be asked anxiously.

'Just a hiccup, that's all, Anne,' Candace told her reassuringly. 'We're altering your position to give the baby more space, and then one of the doctors will have a look at you.'

She wasn't going to tell Anne Burton, whose family had a dairy produce stall on the open air market, that her longed for first child was in grave danger. . .not yet.

As Debbie dashed off to find one of the obstetricians, Candace kept the protruding part of the cord moist with sterile wet saline dressings, and at the same time tried to keep the patient in a relaxed state.

When Gordon came hurrying into the ward, his usual lethargy absent for once, Candace found herself wishing it had been Zac who had answered the emergency, if only for a brief moment of contact with him, but he had promised to stay away from her, and so far it seemed to be working out that way.

'Immediate Caesarean section,' Gordon said in a low voice after he had examined the position of foetus and cord, and as he moved away from the bed, 'any compression on the cord and we could lose the foetus. Get her ready for Theatre, Nurse, and let's hope that the cord isn't looped around the neck.'

It was. Within minutes Anne Burton had been transferred to Theatre, and with two staff nurses assisting, Gordon Grampion made a midline incision which revealed that the cord *was* looped around the baby's neck, and until it had been freed complete delivery would be hindered. Candace found herself tensing. The baby was still at risk, and she held her breath as Gordon carefully eased the cord over the infant's head. Once it was free, they all sighed with relief, and as Candace, holding out a sterile towel, received the wrinkled baby girl from Gordon, she gave her first cry.

Looking down on the unconscious mother, Candace thought that *her* joy had yet to come. She had been put to sleep in a state of great anxiety, but would be waking up to delight.

Zac stayed away from her until Friday night. As she was getting into her car to drive home from the hospital he came up from behind and said quietly, 'Well, have I redeemed myself?'

'Yes, I suppose so,' she said, as her heart began to beat faster.

He smiled properly for once, his eyes lighting up, his mouth softening, and to her amazement asked, 'Can I redeem myself further by taking you for a drive tomorrow?'

Candace goggled at him.

'Where? Over Beachy Head?'

'No,' he said solemnly. 'It would be a mystery tour.'

'Anywhere around here would be a mystery tour to me,' she reminded him. 'Remember I come from the wealthy south, as if you'd ever forget.'

He wagged an admonishing finger.

'Who's making the snide remarks now? But we're getting away from the subject. Will you come? I don't promise a picnic basket, that's not my scene, but I think I can manage a couple of cans and some crisps. . . and a nice meal at the end of it.'

Candace found herself smiling, but, determined not

to be too enthusiastic, she made a show of not being sure, and then said slowly, 'Yes, all right, then. What time do you want me to be ready?'

'Tennish OK? I'll call for you, and now I must go. I'm dining at Kate's.'

'Oh, I see,' she said flatly. 'Bye, then.' And she swung her long legs into the driving seat of the car, wishing she had not been so eager to agree to his suggestion.

When Saturday morning came, Candace didn't know whether to dress up or down for her day out with Zac. If she dressed up too much, he might risk another row and make a comment. On the other hand, if she dressed down too much, she would be uncomfortable because she wasn't looking her best, and so she compromised with a light blue cotton shirt that had cost the earth a few years ago, and white tailored trousers that clung to her slender waist and buttocks with a smoothness that left no doubt about her sensuality.

As she went down the path to meet him, hair flowing loose and golden instead of in its usual coils, his eyes told her that he approved, but his greeting was casual to the extreme.

'Hi. Hop in,' he said, and once she was settled he zoomed off.

The occasions when they had been bodily close had been few, but they'd had the same effect on her as now. Every inch of her was aware of him, the lean brown arms covered in dark hair, the strong capable hands on the wheel, and the dark unforgettable face set in purposeful lines that made her wonder why he had asked her to spend the day with him.

When she saw the gorse-covered slopes of the hills ahead of them, and the road signs for Derbyshire,

Candace stiffened in her seat, and watching her he said evenly, 'What's wrong?'

'You're taking me in to Derbyshire,' she breathed. 'Why?'

'There's someone I want you to meet,' he said in the same measured tones.

'Who?'

He smiled.

'I think you'd better wait and see.'

'Kate says you've got a woman somewhere out here,' she said recklessly. 'That you're on the point of making a commitment to her.'

He frowned.

'Does she, now? It's quite clear that she's been listening to garrulous Gordon. I'm not secretly committed to any *woman*, Candace,' he said gravely. 'Do you understand?'

She was eyeing him in disbelief.

'You don't mean it's a man?'

He laughed, and there was pure amusement in it.

'You're on the right track, but, as I said, wait and see.'

She let out a deep breath.

'You're impossible, Zac, and the most irritating man I've ever met!'

When they stopped outside a large house in the centre of a pretty Derbyshire town built largely from local limestone, Candace knew it had to be the one Gordon Grampion had described. There were well-kept gardens in the front and a short drive, and as they drove up she saw a board with gilt lettering on it almost obscured by mature trees.

At the front door Zac stopped the car and turned to face her.

'What is this place, Zac?' she asked slowly.

He didn't answer. In the shadows of the car his face looked haggard, and if it had been anybody else she would have thought he was nervous.

He opened the car door and she followed suit, and as they stood together on the drive, Candace had the strangest feeling that this was going to be a moment she would remember for a long time.

Children's voices were coming from round the back, loud shrieks of laughter from the abandon of young ones at play, and her eyes widened.

Zac nodded to where the noise was coming from and, taking her hand, he led her round the back of the house. It opened out on to a play area where swings, slides, climbing frames and various other outdoor activities for small bodies were arranged. As she took in the scene, Candace saw that a group of children dressed in bright T-shirts and shorts were playing happily together.

His eyes went over them quickly, and his grip on her hand tightened as his glance went farther afield, and then she felt him relax. A pair of thin brown legs were dangling from one of the lower forks of a huge tree, and the eyes that belonged to them were observing them through the swathes of green leaves.

'I asked you what this place was, Zac,' she said carefully.

His eyes had been still on the tree, but now he swivelled to face her.

'What does it look like, Candace?'

'A children's home.'

'Correct. It's a local authority children's home.'

Light was breaking.

'The one that *you* were in?'

'No. That was about a mile from here. It was

demolished two years ago and they transferred to this place.'

Some of it was becoming clear.

'So why. . .?'

Her question again remained unanswered as at that moment a voice said from behind them, 'Zac! We wondered if you'd be coming today.'

As they turned towards the sound of the voice, Candace saw a pretty dark-haired woman coming towards them with a laundry basket full of wet clothes and pegs under her arm.

'Hi, Jenny,' he said, the constraint still in him. He pulled Candace forward gently. 'This is Candace.'

'Ah, yes. . .Candace,' she said with a friendly smile. 'So Zac has brought you to see us?'

'Er. . .yes,' she admitted awkwardly, aware that her companion was looking somewhat red-faced.

'Have you seen him?' Jenny asked. 'He's around somewhere.'

Zac's smile was brighter than before.

'Yes, he's halfway up the oak tree.'

The woman, Jenny, laughed.

'That one seems to have monkey's blood in him. He's always climbing.'

The sound of running footsteps came from behind them, but they halted abruptly as the three adults turned round, and Candace saw a small boy surveying them with hostile eyes. Zac moved towards him and the boy stood his ground defiantly.

'Hello, Marcus,' he said breezily. 'I'll bet it was great up that tree.'

The small face almost broke into a smile, but he thought better of it, and mumbled offhandedly, 'Wasn't bad,' and then, 'Have you come to take me out?'

'Yes, that's if you want to come. There'll be three of us today. I've brought Candace.'

That brought a scowl.

'She your girlfriend?'

'She *is* a friend, yes,' Zac told him, 'and I'm sure she'll enjoy meeting you.'

'Why should she?'

'Because I say so,' he said, giving him a playful push. 'Go and get a jacket and we'll be off, as long as it's all right with Jenny?'

'Fine by me,' she said. 'Marcus is a different child since you came on the scene. No one seemed to be able to get through to him before.' She turned to Candace. 'He's always in trouble. Nothing criminal, mind you, except a bit of minor thieving, but he was so withdrawn and aggressive until Zac started giving up his precious free time for him. If he's willing to continue to do so we might just end up with a well-adjusted small boy in the end, and that would be marvellous.'

Candace felt a lump come up in her throat, and a cleansing tide of relief washed over her. So this was Zac's commitment in Derbyshire. . .a surly, possibly parentless small boy. It wasn't hard to understand why he'd got involved with him. Did he see himself in the defiant Marcus?

They spent the day in the beautiful countryside near Avonlea, and as Candace watched Zac with the boy, all her annoyances with him were swept away. How could she be uptight with a man who had taken a deprived child under his wing, and in a short space of time had healed some of the scars in his young mind?

As they had driven off from the home with Marcus in the back seat, deep into an adventure comic that

Zac had produced from the glove compartment, she asked in a low voice, 'How old is he, Zac?'

His jaw had tightened.

'In years, or experience?'

'Years.'

'Seven.'

'And his parents?'

'Father unknown, probably didn't even know he'd fathered a child. Mother took a fatal overdose, and the boy was left high and dry in bedsit land. After being passed around like a parcel he was lucky to end up with Jenny and her dedicated team at Avonlea.'

'And how did *you* come to be involved in all this?' she asked quietly.

'You remember I was on two weeks' leave when you started at Montrose? Well, I'd promised myself some walking in the Pennines, and one day I found myself in Derbyshire. I had a sudden urge to see the place where I'd spent my childhood. I'd never been near it since I was sixteen, never wanted to, but on this particular day it was as if something was compelling me to go there. But when I arrived, I discovered that the place had been demolished some years previously, and the land turned into a park. An old fellow sunning himself on one of the benches told me they'd moved to a place called Avonlea not far away. That was it as far as I was concerned, it was only *my* old home I'd wanted to see, but as I made my way out of the area I saw the house in front of me. . .Avonlea. Even then it wouldn't have made any difference until my eyes lit on a small boy sitting on the garden wall, shoulders hunched, and a scowl on his face, and it took me back.

'At that moment Jenny came out to call him in for tea. We got talking, and that was how it all began. Marcus and I. . .an attraction of misfits.'

'Don't say that,' she protested. 'What happened to you was not your fault.' She sighed. 'Three of us with no family to speak of. . .a gathering of orphans.'

Zac had opened his mouth to speak but she put her fingers over his lips. 'I know what you're going to say. . .that *I* didn't do too badly out of it. Well, it's true, I didn't, but I still lost Mum, Dad and Camilla.'

It was Zac's turn to sigh.

'I wasn't going to say anything of the kind, Candace. I was going to ask you what would be your opinion if I decided I wanted a permanent place in Marcus's life.'

She became very still. Why ask *her*? And what did he mean by permanent? Fostering? Adoption? She took a deep breath. If Zac married, it would have to be a very special woman who would be willing to take on a stand-in father and a mixed-up child.

Could *she* do it? she asked herself. Yes, if she loved the man enough, but at this moment in time the question didn't arise. It probably never would, but he was waiting for an answer.

'I'd say that you had some guts and a whole lot of love inside of you that's been going to waste,' she told him, in the knowledge that the last part of her answer had been the truest thing she had ever said. 'But why ask *my* opinion?'

He swallowed, and gave a quick glance over his shoulder to where Marcus had slung the comic and was munching on a packet of sweets.

'Well, you're here, and available,' he said, not meeting her eyes.

'Yes, but why don't you ask Kate what she thinks?' she suggested crisply. 'I know that she's concerned about you.'

His head jerked up.

'In what way?'

'Thinks you're making a mistake by getting involved like this.'

'It's what *you* think that I need to know,' he said, and her heart began to lift. 'After all, as you've just pointed out, we're all three orphans, so you, of all people, should understand how I feel.'

Her heart sank back to its previous level. So her opinion mattered only in as much as *she'd* been deprived of family life too. He wasn't asking because she was special, and having Marcus in his life might affect her too.

They lunched at a farmhouse on the moors, and afterwards when Zac and the boy were kicking a ball about in the field behind it, Candace, watching them, thought what a strange and disturbing day it was turning out to be.

She didn't know why Zac had taken her to Avonlea to meet Marcus, but she was glad that he had, and amazed to discover that the imagined love-nest was a children's home. It was understandable him wanting to do something for the boy, and once Zac knew Marcus better, considering a more permanent relationship, but how would he cope? It wouldn't be fair to the child to take him away from Avonlea to the one-bedroomed flat of a busy doctor who worked long hours. Somebody would have to mind him, and, that being the case, it would be moving him from one sort of restriction to another. All right, he would have the father that he'd never had, but boys needed a mother too, and if Zac wasn't intending filling that gap, it wouldn't be right to move him away from Jenny and the other housemothers.

When they came in from the field, Marcus was doubled up with laughter because Zac had stepped in a cow pat, and Candace thought he seemed no different from any other little boy, until, when they were leaving the farm restaurant, she saw him pocket a tip that had been left on one of the tables. Zac had seen it too, and made him put it back, and the scowl was back along with a mouthful of choice language.

Their eyes met above his dark curls.

'We've quite a long way to go yet, I think,' Zac said with a wry smile, and for a blissful moment it felt as if the 'we' might include herself.

'You're very quiet,' he said as they drove back to the home with a sleepy Marcus curled up on the back seat.

'Yes, I know,' she admitted. 'I'm trying to think how to answer your question. It isn't easy.'

'It could be,' he said without taking his eyes off the road, and then with a quick change of subject, 'Do you remember me telling you how I'd been out on the moors all night?'

'Yes, of course I do. I wondered what you'd been up to.'

'Nothing pleasurable, I assure you. I was looking for Marcus, along with most of the local police force. I'd taken him out once, and on my next visit the car broke down and I was very late. I wasn't anywhere near a phone, so I couldn't ring the folks at Avonlea to explain what had happened.

'Jenny told me afterwards that he sat hunched on the wall waiting for me all afternoon. When she went to bring him in for tea he couldn't be found. By the time I got there, it was panic stations, and we spent all night searching for him. We got back at dawn, and as we tried to eat some breakfast somebody asked if we'd looked in the car boots.

'He was there, in Jenny's car, in the boot, fast asleep, his face all blotchy with weeping, and it was then I knew I had to make sure he wasn't hurt again. Do you understand?'

'Of course I do,' she said softly, 'but, like Kate, I don't think it will be easy. You need to give what you're contemplating a lot of thought. He needs a mother as well as a father, Zac. For his sake don't rush into anything.'

He nodded sombrely.

'You're right, I suppose, but has the woman been created who would feel like coping with Marcus and me? Could I foist a ready-made family on to a woman I loved?'

Candace had had enough. What was he doing, turning the knife? Or did he really not know that she loved him, that she would take on a houseful of children if that was what he wanted? But no doubt he saw her as the last one to cope with a situation like that. . .not the poor little rich nurse.

When they'd handed a sleeping Marcus into Jenny's waiting arms they drove home in the warm summer night. The setting sun was tipping the peaks with rose hue, and the birds and wildlife scurried amongst the hedges in the gloaming. As they came down from the hills and into Cheshire Zac said, 'Are you angry that I involved you in all this? That you've had to spend the day with a difficult small boy?'

'No, of course not,' she told him. 'Marcus wasn't all that difficult.' As far as she was concerned the day had been well spent. She had no regrets whatsoever, for hadn't Zac shown her who it was that he was involved with in a pretty Derbyshire town, shown her that he was twice the man she had thought he was? It was just a pity that his opinion of *her* wasn't as high.

CHAPTER SEVEN

RELUCTANT for the day to end, when they got back to her apartment Candace asked Zac in for coffee, but he shook his head.

'No, Candace, I feel you've had enough of me today. I sprang Marcus on you, which perhaps I shouldn't have done, and you ended up spending the day with a child that you didn't know. Now I feel that I should give you some breathing space.'

She turned her head away, wanting to tell him she didn't need breathing space, that she wanted her life to be full. . .full of him. But that wasn't what he meant, was it? He wanted to give her time to adjust to the fact that he was considering fostering or maybe adopting Marcus. Yet he must be aware that unless she was involved in his plans it was no concern of hers.

She was in love with him, hadn't been able to help herself. He had been in her blood ever since the ill-fated Christmas dinner dance all those years ago. But it seemed that his feelings fell short of what she wanted of him. He thought her beautiful, he'd said so, but he was wary of her. . .and critical, and although it enraged her because it wasn't deserved, it also hurt her deeply. She didn't begrudge Marcus Zac's affection, but as she had asked herself before, why had he none to spare for her? His patients, his friends, an orphaned small boy, he had more than enough warmth to give *them*, but what about her? Was she to go through life carrying a begging bowl?

They were standing on her porch in moonlight that

was turning the long sweep of her hair into silver and making his dark eyes glitter. It could have been a magical moment, but it wasn't, because Zac was brushing her cheek with his lips and turning to go. Desperate to keep him for a little longer, she asked, 'Will you be seeing Marcus tomorrow?'

He paused.

'No. I'm going to have a lie-in, do some thinking, and give my flat the once-over. And you?'

'The same, I imagine, but without the thinking. It can be a disastrous pastime.'

His hand was on the gate,

'Yes, but sometimes it's necessary.'

After he had gone, Candace lay in the warm darkness of her bedroom and knew that sleep was a long way off. The day's events were too uppermost in her mind. . .too vivid. Pictures of Zac with the boy, Zac scouring the moors for him, Marcus on the forecourt of the farm, scuffing his shoes against a stone wall and glowering at them because he'd been made to put the money back, the nice woman, Jenny, hanging out the washing, and her own delight and bewilderment when Zac had let her into his secret.

As they were driving home he had said casually, 'I'd rather you didn't mention Marcus to anyone at Montrose, apart from Kate, who has an inkling of what's going on, not until I've made a decision.' He had turned his head and smiled at her. 'OK?'

'Yes, of course,' she had said immediately. 'It's your affair entirely, and I'm not in the habit of gossiping.'

He had eyed her consideringly for a moment and then said, 'No, I don't imagine you are,' and that coming from Zac was praise indeed.

'I'm trying to decide what to call my daughters,' Janet McCready said when Candace stopped by her bed on Monday morning. 'Lillian is taken care of, but I'm undecided about the other two. I thought that perhaps my favourite nurse might help me choose their names.'

'Me?' Candace said, surprised. 'I'd love to, but it's such a personal thing, naming a child. Wouldn't you and your husband prefer to choose them together?'

Janet laughed.

'Alex is so ecstatic I could call them salt, pepper, and vinegar and he'd beam his approval. No, he's left it to me, and apart from Lillian which is in memory of my mother, I'm looking for two nice names. So any suggestions would be welcome.'

'My sister died in this hospital some years ago,' Candace told her. 'She was my twin. We were very close, and *she* had a lovely name.'

'What was it?' Janet asked, immediately interested.

'Camilla.'

She clapped her hands.

'Why, that's lovely! Camilla it is for my first-born, and perhaps you'd be her godmother, Candace?'

Candace stared at her.

'Are you sure?'

'Positive,' she beamed. 'Will you do it?'

'Yes, I'd be delighted,' and she was. A new baby named after Camilla, and she its godmother.

When Zac came on the unit later in the morning Candace told him blithely, 'I'm going to be godmother to one of Janet's triplets, and guess what?'

He looked tired and low-spirited, but he managed a moderate show of interest.

'What?'

'She's going to call the baby Camilla! Isn't that lovely?'

Her eyes were sparkling like twin sapphires and her mouth was soft with pleasure. He eyed her gravely.

'That makes you really happy, doesn't it?'

'Yes, it does, Zac. There seem to be so few people who need me for anything.'

'What about the patients?' he said, sidetracking the opening she had just given him.

'Yes, well, of course *they* do. I was referring to my personal life.'

He studied her for a moment without speaking, and nodded as if to humour her, then picked up the sheaf of notes from the bottom of the nearest patient's bed and began to glance through them, and watching him Candace saw that he was very pale.

'Are you all right?' she asked.

'I've felt better.'

'I warned you about doing too much thinking,' she said lightly, determined not to be deflated.

'My thinking was soon done. The decisions I made were foregone conclusions.'

And by the looks of it, he was not about to enlighten her as to what they were, she thought dejectedly, as her frail bubble burst.

'And I'm sure it wasn't to blame for the blinding headache and stiff neck that are bugging me,' he said flatly.

That triggered off alarm inside her. He really didn't look his usual energetic and decisive self.

'So you're not well?'

He shrugged.

'It'll pass. I'm rarely ill. Never had to consult a GP in my life,' and, having satisfied himself about whatever he had come for, he went on his way, leaving her with a niggling feeling of unease.

She saw him again later in the day. Gail Saunders,

who worked in the personnel section of Montrose, had been hospitalised for some week after being admitted to the unit in the later stages of pregnancy with painless bleeding from the vagina. Ultrasound scanning had shown that the placenta was attached to the lower part of the uterus instead of to the upper part where it should have been. Some moderate to severe degree of placenta praevia was present, in that the placenta could prevent access for the baby in labour. However bed-rest on the ward had so far contained the problem and she was now allowed up for a short period each day.

Zac had arranged to bring the baby at thirty-eight weeks' gestation, and there was just one week to go, but later that afternoon, after having walked her husband to the main door of the hospital after visiting, she had collapsed in the corridor with severe bleeding, a sure sign that the placenta was coming away and depriving the baby of oxygen.

'She'll need a blood transfusion,' he told Kate when he had examined her. 'The blood loss has put her in shock—note the rapid, shallow breathing, the clammy skin and dizziness. It will have to be brought up to strength, and the Caesarean I was planning for next week will have to be today in a situation like this.'

He sounded weary and Candace eyed him anxiously as Kate went to carry out his instructions. He was still very pale, and she thought that he should be at home instead of having a couple of hours in Theatre ahead of him.

'Couldn't someone else deal with this?' she said in a low voice. 'You don't look at all well.'

He gave a tired grin. 'There *are* times when I've felt better, but I can cope with this.'

'What about infection?' she asked levelly.

'Yes, there's always a high risk of it in these cases.'

'I mean, from yourself.'

He frowned thoughtfully.

'You mean that I might be sickening for something and could pass it on to Gail? I suppose it's possible, and in that case it wouldn't be fair to her, but Rowland is on the golf course this afternoon and Gordon's got quite a lot on his plate.'

'Well, Rowland will have to forgo his pitch and putt, then, won't he,' she said tartly, 'if you're not well?'

'Yes, you're right,' he said with sudden resolve. 'I'll get his secretary to ring the clubhouse, it's only down the road, he can be here in a matter of minutes, and I'll do the sensible thing for once by taking myself off home.'

'That *is* the sensible thing,' she assured him. 'You won't be serving either the patients or yourself by staying, in the state you're in.'

'I know. I'm going,' he said, and as he walked away the unease inside her was increasing.

'Where's Zac?' Kate questioned when she came back. 'Theatre?'

'No,' Candace told her. 'He's gone home because he's not feeling well. He said he was going to ask Mr Ashley's secretary to get hold of him to do Gail's Caesarean section.'

'Fine,' Kate said briskly, 'just as long as somebody is available to operate. If the placenta is breaking away, we've got an at-risk baby and a mother who is going to be feeling far from well, and it's our job to see that they come to no harm.'

She had not shown much concern over Zac, Candace thought, which was strange if they were as close as she imagined them to be, but then, as she had just pointed out, they had a tricky situation on their hands, and that had to be uppermost in both their minds.

'And so what is it that has cost me an afternoon's golf?' Rowland Ashley asked mildly when he appeared in Theatre within minutes of Zac's departure.

'Placenta praevia,' Kate told him as he scrubbed up. 'The mother is one of our own staff here at Montrose, Gail Saunders. She's been confined to bedrest for some weeks and was doing satisfactorily, but just a short time ago everything went haywire and she's feeling quite poorly.'

'Let's get the baby out, then,' he said. 'A quick delivery should benefit them both. There's always trouble ahead when the placenta develops a mind of its own.'

Two hours later, Gail was regaining consciousness back on the ward, and the baby, delivered safely, was being kept in neonatal for observation, and, that being accomplished, Candace found her anxiety over Zac surfacing once more.

As she ate her evening meal, she kept remembering how pale he had been, and she began to worry that he might be ill with no one to care for him. After pacing the apartment for most of the evening, she finally gave in to anxiety, and grabbing a jacket and her car keys she drove round to his flat.

She was dreading making a fool of herself. If he came to the door all bright-eyed and perky, her relief would be mixed with mortification at having to explain why she had come. It was easy to imagine his lip curling and the familiar sardonic gleam in his eyes. He might even think the visit was a follow-on to the remark she had made about not being needed.

She rang the bell, but there was no answer, and was on the point of turning away when she realised that the door wasn't locked, which was strange. Surely he wouldn't go out and leave the place open? Deciding that it was more likely to mean that he was in, rather than out, she pushed it open and went in.

Silence met her for the first few seconds, and then she heard a low groan and she stiffened in alarm. It was obvious that he wasn't out, and as she slowly pushed the bedroom door back she saw him slumped on the bed fully clothed. She was beside him in a flash. He appeared to be in a feverish doze, and when she touched his skin it felt hot and dry. Candace pulled back the drawn curtains to get a clearer look at him and he screwed up his eyes as if the light hurt.

'Zac,' she said anxiously. 'It's me, Candace. Can you hear me?'

He didn't answer and she knew that he needed more experienced help than hers, and covering him with the duvet she said, 'I'm going to get a doctor, my darling.'

She phoned John Airdrie, the elderly GP that Mary Summers worked for, and told him what was wrong.

'Zac told me that he's not registered with a GP,' she told him, 'but he certainly needs to be seen by someone.'

'I'll come over immediately,' he said, and she breathed a sigh of relief.

Zac's condition was unchanged when he arrived, but when the elderly GP began to examine him he opened his eyes, and Candace moved back into the shadows.

'Hello, John,' he said in vague surprise. 'What are *you* doing here?'

'I've come to sort you out, young man,' he said briskly.

'Who sent for you?' Zac mumbled. 'Kate?'

Candace clenched her hands. It was only to be expected that *her* name wouldn't have sprung to his lips. John Airdrie glanced at her quickly, and as if sensing an undercurrent he said easily, 'Never mind who sent for me, just be glad that they did. Now tell me exactly how you feel.'

'Ghastly,' he said with a grimace. 'My head is banging, I can't move my neck, and I'm burning up. I've been vomiting, too.'

'I'm going to have you admitted to Montrose,' he told him. 'They'll do a lumbar puncture, and then we'll soon know if it's a bad dose of flu or. . .'

'Meningitis?' Zac interrupted grimly.

'It's no use trying to kid you, Zac,' he admitted. 'It could be, but let them do the tests first.'

Candace sank down on to the nearest chair. The thought had been at the back of her mind, too, and now they had put it into words her anxiety had changed to fear.

She got to her feet and slipped quietly out of the room, and in the hallway picked up the phone to dial for an ambulance. It seemed crazy when the hospital was only a couple of hundred feet away, but there was no way they could get Zac there under his own steam.

As she was putting the receiver down John Airdrie asked from behind her in a low voice, 'How long has he been like this?'

'I don't know exactly,' she told him. 'I saw him on the unit this afternoon and he didn't look at all well, and because I was concerned about him I came round tonight and found him much worse.'

'I imagine they'll give Zac Chloramphenicol until they've got CSF culture results. If it's viral meningitis there should be no special cause for alarm. If it proves to be meningococcal, then he's in trouble,' he said.

Terror clutched at her heart. When they went back into the bedroom Zac looked so ill she couldn't wait for the ambulance to arrive.

'It's like taking coals to Newcastle,' he mumbled as

they stretchered him out of the flats and into the waiting vehicle, and as Candace and John Airdrie followed there was dread inside her.

She had already lost one person that she loved in the intensive care unit at Montrose. She couldn't cope with losing another. . .not Zac of the strong mind and even stronger principles. The dark avenger who had twice told her he didn't know why he used her as a verbal punchbag. Zac, who saw his own young nightmare reflected in that of an awkward small boy and wanted to do something about it. . .and Zac who'd had Kate's name on his lips back there in the flat.

It was a long, harrowing night that reminded her of the night they had brought Camilla into this same part of the hospital, and there was a horrible feeling of repetition about it.

They'd given Zac the antibiotic that John had said they would, followed by a lumbar puncture, and now it was a matter of waiting for the results from tests on the organisms from the culture growth, which would take until the following day.

Candace sat beside him as he slept fitfully, until the dawn streaked across the summer sky, and then she knew that she would have to leave him to prepare for another day on the unit.

'I'm on the maternity unit,' she told the nurse in charge. 'Please let me know if there is any further cause for alarm.'

The girl smiled.

'Sure will. We can't have anything happening to Zac Stephens. I couldn't believe my eyes when they brought him in. He always looks so fit. I'd have thought he was bacteria-proof.'

Candace smiled wearily. 'It's the fit who pick up the

bugs. Creaking gates are usually so full of minor bacteria that the really vicious germs can't get a hold.'

'Yes,' she agreed. 'Like cancer. . .it likes a clear field to attack.'

As Candace tried to force down some breakfast, the day ahead loomed frighteningly. It was incredible to think of Zac limp and ill from what might be a life threatening condition.

'What's this I hear about Zac?' Kate asked anxiously when she arrived on the unit. 'John Airdrie phoned to say that he'd had him admitted into Intensive Care last night with suspected meningitis. I'm on my way to see him now.'

'Yes, it's true,' Candace told her. 'He wasn't at all well yesterday afternoon, and I was worried about him all evening. In the end I went round to his flat, and when I saw him I sent for John.'

'Good for you. I wonder where he's picked it up from. It's more common during the winter months.'

Candace shook her head.

'I don't know. I suppose we in health care are all open to infection. We'll just have to hope that it's viral.'

Kate was eyeing her thoughtfully.

'Are *you* all right? I expect you've been up half the night.'

She'd been up *all* the night, and knew she wouldn't sleep until Zac was out of danger. . .and if that didn't happen. . .what then? She would be for ever sleepless.

When Kate came back she said, 'He was awake, and seemed to think it was I who sent for John.'

'What did you say?'

Kate gave her a knowing smile.

'I told him to think about it, and he'd soon realise who it was.'

Candace went to see him the moment she came off duty, and found him looking even worse than the night before, as now there was dark stubble on his pale face. He was scrutinising his chest and arms and when he saw her he said in morose greeting, 'There aren't any red blotches so far.'

'That's good, then,' she said, wishing he'd found time to say hello.

'Not necessarily. They don't always appear.'

She was determined not to get rattled.

'Is that so?' she said mildly. 'Well, one thing is for sure, you'll soon know.'

He moved his head restlessly on the pillow.

'Am I in your debt?'

She eyed him warily.

'It depends what you mean.'

'I mean that were *you* responsible for bringing John out to me?'

'Yes. *I* phoned him,' she said calmly, as if finding the man she loved in such a state was all part of a day's work. 'I'm sorry if you disapprove.'

He frowned.

'Did I say that? But I can't stay here, Candace,' he said raggedly. 'There's too much to do on the unit. . . and what about Marcus?'

'Zac,' she said patiently, 'it's only Tuesday. You see Marcus at the weekends, and you could be feeling much better by then.'

'Not this week,' he said tetchily. 'There's going to be a circus on a field not far from Avonlea tomorrow night, and I've promised to take him.'

'I'll phone Jenny and explain what's happened,' she offered. 'She'll understand.'

'*She* might,' he said morosely, 'but Marcus won't. He'll think I make promises and don't keep them.'

He raised himself up on to one elbow, and now he sank back dejectedly against the pillows.

'Zac, it's no use upsetting yourself about the circus,' she said firmly. 'There'll be another time. You've not been brought into this place for nothing, you know. I *will* phone Avonlea and talk to Jenny. I promise.'

He had to be satisfied with that, and looking around him morosely he said, 'This is *not* my scene, Candace.'

'I'm afraid that it has to be for the moment,' she told him with a hard won calm. 'You're ill, and until we know just how ill, you'll have to stay put.'

He closed his eyes.

'OK, I know,' and then, 'Has John given *you* any antibiotics? It's all very well putting on a mask and gown when you come in here, but you were with me at the flat, and God knows I don't want *you* to pick up this ghastly thing, whatever it is.'

'Yes, he has. He thought it a bit late to think of vaccination, and so antibiotics it is.'

There was a glow inside her because Zac was concerned about her, but it dwindled as she told herself that he would be just as concerned about anyone else who had been near him.

When Candace got back to her apartment she immediately rang Avonlea, and Jenny said, 'Oh, dear! I *am* sorry. I do hope it won't turn out to be too serious.'

I'll go along with that, Candace thought wretchedly, and told her, 'Zac is concerned that Marcus will feel that he's let him down because he won't be taking him to the circus tomorrow night.'

'Yes, I'm not surprised that he's upset,' Jenny said, 'but it's not his fault, is it? Tell him not to worry. *I'll* explain to Marcus.'

'Before you do,' Candace said, 'tell me something.

Has he by any chance been vaccinated against meningitis?'

'Yes, as a matter of fact he has,' the young house-mother said. 'There was a mini epidemic of it around here on the tail end of the winter, and in a home such as this, anything infectious spreads like a forest fire. All the children were done.'

'Ah! Well, in that case *I'll* take him to the circus. I don't need to worry about passing it on to him. I know I'll be a poor substitute for Zac, but at least Marcus won't feel so let down.'

'Are you sure?' Jenny asked at the other end of the line. 'It's a long way to come after working all day.'

'Yes, I'm sure. What time does it start?'

'Seven.'

'I'll be at your place for half past six, then.'

'Fine. I'll go and tell him the bad news and the good news in that order.' She laughed. 'It will be interesting to see how he takes to the change of plan.'

'Yes, I think you're right,' Candace said wryly, and asked herself which of them was she trying to please. . . the boy or the man? Both of them, obviously. But it was Zac, ill and miserable, who was at the forefront of her mind.

She had decided that she would tell him that *she'd* taken Marcus to the circus when they had been. That way, if he had any disturbing comments to make, it wouldn't be so bad because the deed would be done.

The next day she went to see him in her lunch hour and his first question was, 'Did you phone Avonlea?'

'Yes. I said I would, and I did. Jenny said not to worry. She'll talk to Marcus.'

He sighed and she took his hand in hers.

'Fair enough. I suppose I can't expect any better than that,' he said, and then his face lightened. 'At least I've had some good news this morning. The results of the tests have come through and it's viral, the least serious of the three. I'm still feeling very rough physically, but mentally I'm on cloud nine, except for the fact that it could be two to three weeks before I'm clear of it and on my feet again, which is a sickener.'

Candace laughed. It was as if a huge weight had been lifted off her heart.

'Sick being the significant word,' she gurgled, and Zac managed a smile.

'The staff keep badgering me to think back to where I might have picked up the virus,' he said. 'It can be caught from a neonate, of course, but there haven't been any such cases recently. The only thought that springs to mind is that I've had an ear infection in the last few weeks, and it's possible for bacteria to get through cavities in the skull and cause meningitis.'

'Wherever it's come from, be glad that it's only a mild form,' she said tremulously, at the thought of the horror now past.

He nodded. 'To say I'm relieved is putting it mildly.'

Candace glanced at her watch. 'I have to go, Zac. My lunch hour is up.'

'Will I see you tonight?' he asked casually.

'Er—no. I have an appointment.'

'That friend from your idle youth?'

'Roddy? No, not Roddy. This young man is taking me to a show.'

'I see. Lucky you.' And he turned over and closed his eyes, hunching his shoulder against her. Candace hesitated. Should she tell him where she was going? It wasn't fair to mislead him, but Zac was hardly likely to be concerned about *her* social life, what there was of it. It was *she* who had been bursting with curiosity about *his*, and what a surprise she'd had awaiting her. Well, she might just have one for him in the morning.

Candace drove into Derbyshire in heavy summer rain, and she thought that unless the circus tent was a sturdy structure the deluge might cause it to be cancelled, and that would be another disappointment for Marcus.

He was ready and waiting when she got to Avonlea, scrubbed clean in a red shirt and dark blue shorts.

'Hello, Marcus,' she said. 'It's just going to be the two of us tonight. Zac isn't well.'

If she had expected an answer, she was to be disappointed. He stared at her with a dubious sort of stillness and then walked past her and went to stand by the car.

'I'll bring him straight back,' she told Jenny, 'and thanks for letting me take him.'

'It's our pleasure,' the young housemother said. 'It's nice to see him so happy and excited.'

Candace eyed him doubtfully.

'That's not exactly the impression *I* get.'

Jenny smiled.

'He's wary, is our little Marcus. He's learned to conceal his feelings, which is sad at so young an age, but the excitement *is* there inside him. He won't let it out until he knows he's on safe ground. He discovered that life isn't always fair when he was very small, and doesn't trust anyone or anything, but don't let him fool you, Candace. He's just as excited as any other seven-year-old underneath.' Feeling still doubtful in spite of Jenny's reassurances, Candace strapped him into the seat beside her and set off.

They had been travelling for several minutes before he spoke, and when he did he hardly sounded like an excited child.

'Is Zac going to die?' he asked, solemn-faced.

Candace swivelled to face him, heart thumping at the unexpected question.

'No, Marcus, he's not going to die,' she told him gravely. 'It might be about three weeks before he's really better, but he's not going to die.'

He was looking down at his shoes.

'My mummy died.'

Candace swallowed.

'Yes, I know she did, but not everyone who has an illness dies from it.'

'She wasn't ill,' he said tonelessly. 'One of the big kids told me it was because she was fed up of me.'

She reached across and took his small hand in hers, thinking that she hadn't bargained for this.

'It wouldn't be you that she was fed up with, Marcus. It would be life in general, and that *is* an illness, but I don't think you should be worrying about it tonight because we're off to the circus, aren't we?'

'So Zac isn't going to die?'

'No, he isn't,' she told him firmly, wondering what was coming next.

'That's OK, then,' he said casually, and she began to relax.

'Good. No more questions?'

He grinned, and she saw that he had lost a front tooth since Saturday.

'Just one.'

Candace hoped it was going to be easier than the last. It was.

'Can I have some popcorn when we get to the circus?'

She laughed.

'Is that all? Of course you can.'

As they joined a long queue of people filing into a

huge marquee, she realised that her fears that the
circus might have been cancelled were groundless. She
took Marcus by the hand to make sure that she didn't
lose him, and half expected him to pull away, but he
didn't, and if it hadn't been for the thought of Zac
lying ill and wretched in Montrose she would have
been looking forward to a most enjoyable evening.

In spite of Zac not being there, and the rain beating
down on the canvas, it *was* an enjoyable evening,
because Marcus was behaving like a normal seven-
year-old, laughing at the clowns, gazing wide-eyed at
the trapeze artists, and enrapt with the noise and smell
of the sawdust. There was another reason, too. She
had done what Zac would have wanted, not perhaps
with herself in the leading role, but he would have
wanted Marcus to see the circus somehow or other,
and she had made it possible.

When they got back to Avonlea, Jenny said, 'What
do you say to Candace, Marcus?'

'Thanks,' he said, in his gruff little boy's voice.

'And haven't we got something for Zac?' Jenny
prompted.

His face lit up.

'Yes.'

'Well, go and get it, then.'

As he ran upstairs, she said, 'It's all his own work. I
got him to do it this afternoon to take his mind off the
disappointment.' She smiled. 'Which doesn't seem to
have been one after all.'

It was a get-well card made out of a piece of white
cardboard, with a childish drawing on the front of a
doctor bending over a patient in bed, and both of them
had a stethoscope around their necks. Inside in a round
unformed hand he had written,

Get well sune, Zac.
Love, Marcus.

'That's lovely, Marcus,' Candace told him as tears came up in her throat. 'I'll give it to him first thing in the morning.'

'Don't forget,' he cautioned, and she nodded meekly.

'I won't forget.'

Zac was staring moodily out of the window when she approached his bed before reporting to the unit the next morning. At the sound of her footsteps he turned his head slowly.

'You're an early bird this morning,' he said. 'Did you have a nice evening with your. . .friend?'

She smiled, and it was like the bright summer sun.

'Yes, lovely.'

'I see.'

'No, you don't, Zachary,' she said with a happy laugh. 'You don't see at all.'

He glared at her, and she was reminded of Marcus.

'My boyfriend sent this for you,' and she handed him the card.

'Huh?' His expression was even darker. 'What do you mean?'

'Open it, and you'll see. Then you'll know exactly what I'm on about.'

Candace watched his face lighten like the sky after rain, and his incredulous smile was the rainbow.

'You've seen Marcus?'

'Yes.'

'How? Where?'

'I took him to the circus.'

'You did! That's marvellous! I nearly asked you to substitute for me, but didn't think I had the right.'

'You had every right,' she told him softly, 'but you didn't need to ask. I knew how much it meant to you both.'

His eyes were melting with pleasure, vitality pouring back into him as he said huskily, 'If I hadn't got this damned virus, I'd kiss you until your cap fell off. . . Nurse.'

Caught up in his mood, she whispered, 'Then you'd better get well soon. . .Doctor.'

'You bet,' he promised.

As the relentless fingers of the clock started moving to the stroke of eight Candace said, 'I'll have to go, Zac. I'll tell you about Marcus and the circus tonight.'

He was smiling and looked so much better.

'I'll look forward to that,' he said, and there was the promise in his eyes of other things to look forward to. . .together.

CHAPTER EIGHT

When Candace saw Zac that evening it was clear that his ebullient mood of the morning hadn't gone away. In fact, he was happier than she had ever seen him, and she felt a strange little pain around her heart.

Was his contentment because Marcus hadn't missed his treat? she wondered. Or was it because she'd redeemed heself by taking him? Or could it possibly be because he now saw her as part of a loving trio? She hoped so.

'And so tell me all about it,' he said with a smile as she seated herself beside his bed. 'But first, am I correct in thinking that you checked that he'd been vaccinated before you went?'

In weeks past she would have bridled at the remark, seen it as the forerunner of some sort of censure, but tonight she could appreciate that he was only asking because he cared. . .for the boy.

'Yes, of course I did,' she told him with an answering smile, and then proceeded to tell him all about the visit to the circus, with one exception. She didn't tell Zac that Marcus had been afraid he was going to die. It would only distress him to know that the child had voiced such a fear.

'I could bring him here to see *you* on Sunday, if you wish,' she offered. 'Pick him up in the morning, give him lunch at my place, and then return him to Avonlea in the early evening. Would you like that?'

'I'd like it very much,' he said immediately. 'I like everything about the idea, but even though Marcus has

133

been vaccinated, I don't want him in here. There are too many strains of this particular virus, and one of them might not react to the vaccine. If you're prepared to spend Sunday with him, Candace, that's great, but I think you'll have to count me out. In any case, he might find it boring hanging around a hospital.'

'I think he would be more likely to find it reassuring than boring,' she told him 'seeing you in the flesh, even if it is only through the window. So I shall bring him, but keep him out of the wards.'

'Are you sure you want to do this?' he questioned. 'Giving up your Sunday?'

'Yes,' she said calmly. 'If it makes you both happy.'

His eyes were searching her face, intense, penetrating, and she felt her cheeks redden.

'What does it take to make *you* happy, Candace?' he asked gravely. 'Do you miss the excitement of life in London?'

'Yes, sometimes,' she told him truthfully, 'but only when I'm low-spirited and feel I need livening up. Or when I have a sudden urge to get a beautiful dress off the hanger. . .and wear it.'

'That was a memorable creation you wore all those years ago,' he said casually.

Candace eyed him in amazement. 'You remember?'

'Of course,' he said simply, as if surprised she should question the fact. 'Camilla's beautiful sister making her entrance at our humble northern Christmas event. The sun goddess had come to the ball.'

Her face tightened.

'If you're going to start. . .'

'I'm not,' he said gently. 'You were the most stunning thing I'd ever seen. . .stunning and disturbing.'

'I would never have known you thought that from the way you've treated me,' she said, dumbfounded.

'Ah, well, we minor mortals have to be on our guard against anything that threatens our equilibrium.'

Her amazement was increasing.

'You're not saying that I made you nervous! I don't believe it!' she said with an incredulous laugh.

'Not nervous. Unsettled would be a better word, and that's a state of mind I can do without. I've been unsettled enough in my life, and just when I'd got it well and truly anchored, who should come along but you?'

Her heart was beating a frantic tattoo against her ribcage, and her mouth had gone dry. Was this the moment she had been suspended in time for? Was Zac going to tell her that he loved her as much as she loved him? Or was it just another instance of letting her see that she was still on the perimeter of his life?

'And how do you see me now?' she asked softly.

'Still as the diverting temptress,' he said with a dry smile, 'but in hospital blue instead of flame silk.'

'And which do you prefer?'

'I like them both, but that is how it will have to stay, I'm afraid.' He saw the disappointment in her eyes and went on to say reassuringly, 'Until I've got rid of this damned virus.'

'Yes, of course,' she agreed, her smile back. 'Until you're well again, Zac.'

Saturday morning started off with a phone call from her uncle to say that his wedding was to be in three weeks' time, and would she still be able to come?

'Yes, of course,' she assured him, 'but I've only been at Montrose long enough to qualify for two days' leave, so it will have to be fly out Friday and come back on a Monday flight, if that's all right with you?'

'Certainly,' he agreed readily, 'though I'd like to see

a little more of you than that, but as long as you're there, that's the main thing. If you want to bring someone along for company, do so, my dear. The wedding will be a very quiet affair. At this end there'll be Margot and myself, of course, her stepson by her marriage to Pedro Garcia, and a couple from Faro and their daughter, who have been friends of hers for a long time, making eight in all, if you bring someone with you.'

After Harry had gone off the phone, Candace sat in thoughtful mood. He had suggested she take a friend. Dared she ask Zac? The thought of a few days alone with him away from Montrose was a delight that needed no contemplating, and the rest, lazing beneath the Portuguese sun, would be beneficial to him after his illness. Her mouth curved softly. There was the answer. Invite him to accompany her to Portugal in the form of a mini convalescence.

Each time she saw him now there was this delicious warmth between them, and she felt sure that if he hadn't been infectious they would have been in each other's arms, but there was one thing they weren't short of, and that was time. She had waited for Zac this long; she could wait a little longer.

On the Saturday night she said casually, 'How would you like a long weekend in Portugal when you get out of here?'

He eyed her in some disbelief.

'I'd like it fine, but what do you mean?'

'My uncle is getting married three weeks today in Monte Gordo. Obviously I'm going to be there for him, even though I've only two days' leave due to me. He suggested that I bring a friend, and I thought of you. A weekend in the sun would help you to recuperate more quickly.'

'I'll recuperate fast enough when I get out of here,' he told her decisively. 'I'm feeling better with each day.'

Candace turned away to hide her dismay. So she had been taking too much for granted. He wasn't bursting to come away with her.

'Fair enough,' she agreed steadily.

'You're not letting me finish,' he said with a quick glance at her set face. 'I'd love to go to Portugal with you. From what I remember of your uncle, he was a very nice guy. I'd be only too pleased to be present at his nuptials.'

Some of the disappointment had gone, but not all of it. He hadn't said that he would be only too pleased to spend some time alone with her. Was she imagining the new rapport between them? His next words showed that maybe she wasn't.

'That will be one weekend when Marcus will *have* to be disappointed,' he said, 'but there'll be many more times to make up for it, won't there, Candace?' and she wasn't going to disagree with that.

She had phoned Avonlea during the latter part of the week to ask if she might bring Marcus to see Zac. It had been Jenny's day off and she'd spoken to a young housefather called Mike, who had assured her that it would be all right, and that he would inform Jenny about the arrangement the next day.

And now, on Sunday morning, she was *en route* once more to Derbyshire. This time there was a warmer welcome for her from Zac's young protégé, and he chattered all the way to Montrose, where she had decided to take him to see Zac before lunch and then again in the afternoon.

He was standing by the window watching for them, his trim physique fined down by the illness, and when

Marcus saw him he galloped away from her across the
grass and pressed his face up against the glass. Zac had
opened the window at the top so that they could hear
each other speak, but it was firmly closed down below.

The boy's eyes were taking in every detail of the
man who had come into his life not so long ago and
changed it, and then they gazed around the room until
they rested on the homemade get-well card in its place
of honour on the bedside table.

Zac smiled as he followed his glance.

'Thanks for the card, Marcus. I really appreciated
it,' he said gravely, and then, 'I'll soon be out of here
and then we'll celebrate, and as Candace is doing all
the running around on our behalf, I think we should
let her choose how. What do you say?'

Marcus swung round to where she was standing a
few steps behind him and smiled his gappy smile.

'Yes, but I can help her choose, can't I?'

Zac laughed.

'Yes, as long as it's not the moon or the north pole.'

They lunched in her apartment, Candace and the
boy, and as he tucked into beefburger and chips she
was filled with tenderness. She and Zac together could
do so much for him, but *her* place in the scheme of
things had yet to be decided, and she hoped that the
weekend in Portugal might do just that.

Most of the afternoon was spent outside Zac's room
with him and Marcus playing at throwing a small rubber
ball, which Zac had produced out of his trouser pocket,
to each other through the open window, while Candace
watched them from a bench nearby.

There had been no hiccups so far with regard to
Marcus, and she was feeling quite complacent about
the day's happenings, until he ran to retrieve the ball
from behind a nearby shrubbery and didn't reappear.

'He's hiding,' she thought languidly as the hot sun beat down upon her resting place, but when she got up and strolled across to look for him, he wasn't there.

Zac was watching her through the window, his smile wiped off, and waving his arms to indicate that she look farther afield. She obeyed, searching quickly through all the bushes, and then around the side of the building, and finally into the corridor that led to where Zac was, but there was no Marcus. Sheer disbelief had her in its grip. The far side of the shrubbery bordered a busy main road; suppose. . .suppose. . .

As she went past Zac's window and met his enquiring eyes, she shook her head, and then she was delving back into the shrubbery, pushing her way through to where railings separated it from the road, and it was then that she saw him, walking away from an ice-cream van with three cornets in his hand. Candace grasped the railings as her legs almost gave way with relief, and when he got up to her, Marcus gave her the ice-creams to hold while he climbed over.

'Mind the spikes,' she cautioned weakly, and he nodded, confidently. Once he was over he took the cones off her and then handed one back, saying casually, 'My treat.'

'And my heart attack almost!' she cried. 'I thought we'd lost you!'

He stared at her.

'Didn't you hear the ice-cream van?'

'What if I did?' she said. 'You should have told me where you were going. That's a very busy road. You could have been knocked down, or kidnapped.'

He met her eyes unblinkingly, a cornet in each hand.

'Nobody's going to kidnap *me*. The cook at Avonlea says I'm too much of a handful for anybody.'

Candace was smiling, the panic receding.

'Zac doesn't think that,' she said, but when they got back to the window he looked as if he could have leapt through it and shaken him, until Marcus proffered the cornet and repeated airily,

'My treat.'

His reaction was the same as her own, amusement taking the edge off his anxious indignation, and as they all sucked their cornets Candace thought that there was never a dull moment with Marcus around.

During the days that followed there was sweet harmony between them, until Roddy showed up one night as Candace was crossing the gardens to visit Zac.

When he called her name she turned, and managing to find a smile she said, 'Hello, Roddy. So you're in the neighbourhood again?'

'Yes, I am,' he replied affably, 'and I wondered if we could perhaps get together once more?'

'I'm afraid not,' she told him. 'I'm otherwise engaged at the moment.'

His affability disappeared.

'Surely not all the time? And what do you mean by otherwise engaged?'

'What I said,' she told him coldly, annoyed by his manner. 'All my free time is taken up visiting someone who is sick. . .with a very infectious illness.'

That had the desired effect. He took a step backwards, and said warily, 'Infectious?'

Candace tried not to smile.

'You've heard of the bubonic plague, haven't you?'

His enthusiasm for her company was disappearing by the minute.

'Yes, well—er—perhaps some other time, eh?' he suggested halfheartedly, and she nodded regally.

'Yes, Roddy, maybe some other time.'

Zac had seen the confrontation from his window, and when she went in he said, 'Was that your London friend, Rodders?'

'It was Roddy Carstairs, yes,' she said stiffly, feeling that it was all right for *her* to have a joke at his expense, but she saw no need for Zac to do the same.

'What did he want?'

'He wanted to take me out.'

'And what did you say?'

'Stop interrogating me, Zac!' she cried, stung into anger. 'That's *my* business.' She wanted to tell him that a thousand Roddys wouldn't keep her away from *him*, but it was as always, anything connected with her past life had to be gibed at. She slammed out of the room and immediately wished she hadn't, but there was no way she was going to be badgered by two of them in one night.

When she saw Zac the next day her anger was long gone, and he said with a quizzical smile, 'Am I forgiven? You shouldn't berate the sick, you know.'

Candace smiled.

'True, but then the sick shouldn't be so stroppy.'

'Point taken,' he said, and harmony between them was restored, even though they were both aware that she hadn't put him in the picture with regard to Roddy.

Zac was discharged at the end of his third week in Montrose, and spent the fourth prowling around his flat, champing at the bit because John Airdrie wouldn't sign him off to go back to work.

'Time enough when you've had this break in Portugal,' he said. 'You're going at the end of the week, aren't you?' and when Zac nodded, 'Well, then, you can get back into harness when you come back, on the condition that you feel up to it.'

'I feel up to it now,' Zac had protested. 'You know what it's like on the unit at the moment with Rowland still wrapped up in his grief, and Gordon useless to say the least.' He sighed. 'However, as I've had an infectious illness I suppose you're probably right in not letting me rush back too soon.'

'What do you mean, probably?' the elderly GP had bellowed with mock ferocity. 'I *am* right! And you'll go back on the wards when your doctor says so. . . Doctor!'

Candace had done the round trip to Derbyshire each Sunday, much to the delight of Marcus. . .and Zac, and when they told the small boy that the next weekend they would be away he had taken the news much more casually than they had expected, and without the usual scowl that appeared when things didn't suit him.

'I've still got the doctor's kit that you bought me,' he told Zac solemnly. 'If they're short-staffed they can give me a bleep.'

'I'll make sure they're aware of that,' Zac told him with equal gravity, and Marcus had smiled his toothless smile.

Janet McCready and her triplets had gone home, and on the morning that she was being discharged she said to Candace, 'I'll be in touch about the christening, Candace. It will be a few weeks before we get round to it, as we want it to be a special occasion, and with three sets of godparents to find, and catering for all our relatives and friends, it's going to take some planning, but I'll contact you as soon as I know when.'

She had a baby on each arm, and her husband was beside her holding the third member of their family and the suitcase with her belongings.

'Thanks again for agreeing to do the honours for my tiny Camilla,' she said, and Candace thought that it was one of the moments of extreme pleasure that went with the job. It was always gratifying to see parents

with one healthy baby to take home, and when it came
to three, it was an event.

'I shall look forward to hearing from you,' she told
Janet, and wondered if by then she would be close
enough to Zac to ask him to accompany her.

That week was a busy one for her, working during
the day, visiting Zac at the flat each evening, and
preparing for the weekend ahead. If she was disappointed that he wasn't keeping to his promise of how it
would be when he was well, she reminded herself that
he had only been home a few days, and that in a short
space of time they would have four whole days
together, and *then* they would make up for lost time.

They were flying to Portugal on the Friday afternoon
and returning Monday evening, and as Candace packed
the clothes she had chosen for the occasion, late on
Thursday night, there was a sense of anticipation inside
her unlike anything she had ever known before.

She had been abroad countless times, but not in
these circumstances, not to be present at a very special
wedding, and not with someone as important to her as
Zac.

When he came to pick her up at the apartment on
Friday lunchtime he eyed her with approval. She was
wearing beige trousers, a cream silk blouse and a long
heavy-knit camel-coloured cardigan, and for coolness
had swept her hair back with a gold clasp.

'Very nice,' he murmured. 'You look what you are.'

'And what is that?' she asked, hoping there was no
sting to the words.

'A beautiful and elegant woman.'

That was music to her ears, and with heightened
colour she gave a tinkling laugh.

'Not when I'm up to my elbows in foetuses and
placentas.'

'Even more so *then*,' he said with a laugh of his own, and picking up her case he waited for her to lock the door, then grabbed her hand and ran with her to the car, obviously in high spirits like herself.

The euphoria inside her lasted all the way to the airport and through the flight, as Zac held her hand and they spent the time alternating between companionable silences and non-stop discussions on every subject under the sun except themselves. Candace told herself to be patient, that this easiness between them wasn't imagined. It was the rapport of those in love, and sooner or later Zac was going to admit it.

It was as the aircraft began its descent at Faro that he said with sudden seriousness, 'I owe you a lot, Candace. You've been there for me while I was ill, brought Marcus to me, and now you're even taking me away for the weekend.' His smile was wry. 'It's a strange feeling for me to be indebted to someone in the course of my adult life. God only knows I was told often enough that I ought to be grateful when I was young, and since then I've always tried to work it that other people owe *me*. That way there are no strings attached.'

At his words Candace came down to earth with a thud.

'And is that how you want it to be with me. . .no strings?' she asked with a dangerous calm.

'At one time I did, yes. I've always found relationships tricky. It comes from community living, I suppose. I've never visualised myself in a one-to-one situation, but. . .'

'But what? ' she croaked.

'But I'd reckoned without meeting a girl in a flame silk dress. For a short time she was like a thorn in my flesh. Then she went away, and I told myself that was good. I hadn't made a fool of myself. I could get on with my life as before, but I hadn't bargained for the effect that your short stay at Montrose had on you. Behold, you were in my life again, in a different mould, but still the same beautiful distraction as before.'

'And so what are you saying?' she asked quietly.

'I'm saying that maybe I don't want to fight it any longer, that when we get back. . .'

To her dismay the rest of the sentence was lost in the whine of the engines as the plane touched down, and as it jolted along the tarmac they were told over the audio system to keep to their seats until it had come to a halt.

By the time the chance came to finish the conversation that had been interrupted by landing they were in the Arrivals area, and as Candace opened her mouth to speak her uncle's voice called from nearby, 'Candace, my dear!'

She swung round and there he was, his craggy face alight with the pleasure of seeing her. At his side was a slim brown-haired woman with bright hazel eyes. Her smile was just as warm, but there was the diffidence of stranger meeting stranger in it. To her dismay, Candace saw that they weren't alone; behind them, with a confident smile on his face, unbelievably and disastrously, was Roddy Carstairs.

As her uncle held her in his arms, Candace could have wept. Roddy's presence was the last thing she had expected or wanted. It was only three weeks since she had given him his marching orders at Montrose, and now he had surfaced again. He was spoiling her reunion with Harry, throwing her off balance at the moment of meeting the woman her uncle was to marry, but worst of all was the daunting thought that the tender buds of her relationship with Zac were not going to burst into flower with Roddy on the scene.

Harry Carson took the hand of his bride-to-be and said proudly, 'Candace, this is Margot. I have waited a long time for her and tomorrow she will make me the happiest man on earth.'

'Hello, my dear,' she said in a low musical voice that had a faint accent. 'Haree has told me so much about you, and now, delightfully, you are here, to share in our wedding.' Her bright hazel gaze had transferred itself to Zac. 'Along with your friend.'

Aware of Roddy's curious eyes, Candace turned and took Zac's hand in hers. It was stiff and inflexible and his fingers didn't wrap around hers as they had on the flight.

'Yes, may I introduce Zachary Stephens,' she said, challenging the coolness in the dark eyes, 'a very special friend of mine?'

'We've met before, I think, though only briefly,' Harry Carson said as he shook Zac's hand and the two men took stock of each other. 'You were there when we lost Camilla, weren't you?'

'Yes. I was,' Zac told him with a smile. 'I was a junior doctor then.'

'And what are you now?' her uncle asked with an answering smile

'An obstetrician.'

'So you're both on the same unit. . .the same hospital?'

'Yes, that's correct,' Zac said evenly.

'It's a small world, isn't it?'

'It is, indeed,' Zac agreed. 'People turn up out of the blue, sometimes unexpectedly, but not always.' And his eyes went to Roddy waiting to be introduced.

'Have you met Roddy Carstairs?' Harry asked. 'He's

an old friend of Candace's who stopped by unexpectedly, and is staying for the wedding.'

'No, I haven't,' Zac told him equably, as if meeting her old boyfriends was the pleasantest pastime on earth. He took Roddy's languidly offered hand and said coolly, 'We haven't met, but I've seen you from a distance a couple of times.'

'Oh? Where was that?' Roddy drawled.

'Montrose Hospital,' Zac told him briefly, and turning back to his host, 'Thank you for inviting me to your home. I picked up a nasty bug some weeks ago and your niece thought that a weekend in the sun, coinciding with a very pleasant occasion, could be beneficial.'

Candace was squirming. Zac was talking as if he had come with her merely to get well. And what was all this 'your niece' business? Why so formal? She had a name.

'It's our pleasure to have you with us, Zachary,' her uncle said affably. 'Isn't it, Margot?'

'It ees indeed, Haree,' she said, placing her hand in the crook of his arm, 'but let us take our guests away from thees place. We do not want to spend the day in the airport, *non*?'

She smiled at Candace, who had been trying to place her accent.

'I am half French, half English, and to complicate matters I married a Portuguese, but tomorrow the English side of me will be the stronger, because I will have got me an English husband,' she said with a loving smile for the man by her side.

As they drove to Monte Gordo with Roddy following in his own car, Candace saw that this was a much more rural area than the parts of Portugal she had visited before. Whole families could be seen toiling on the rich red soil with wide-brimmed straw hats protecting them from the hot sun.

'Why did you choose Monte Gordo?' she asked her uncle as he turned the car on to a coast road that bordered silver sands.

'It's not as commercialised as some parts of the Algarve,' he said, 'and it was near to Faro where a very special lady I'd known in my youth was living, and for that reason alone I would have pitched my tent at the top of Everest if it had been necessary.' And he turned his head to give the woman beside him a doting smile. 'It's practically on the Spanish border,' he went on to explain. 'Vila Real, the town just a couple of miles down this coast road, is actually in Spain.'

At that moment Harry swung the car away from the sea into a tree-lined development of large villas, and as they pulled up at the first one he said over his shoulder, 'Welcome to the Villa Camille,' and as Candace felt a lump come up in her throat, 'we don't forget her, eh, Candace?'

'No, never,' she said chokingly, and if Zac hadn't been sitting silent and withdrawn beside her she would have buried her head against him for comfort.

They had been shown into adjoining rooms at the back of the villa and overlooking the sea, and Margot said from the doorway, 'I will have some light refreshments sent up for the moment, and we dine in one hour's time. *Oui*?'

'That will be fine,' Candace said, and Zac smiled his agreement, but the smile disappeared at the same time as their hostess, and Candace decided that she'd had enough.

'I want to talk to you,' she said decisively. 'You're shutting me out again and I want to know why. If it's because of Roddy Carstairs being here, I can assure you that I was as surprised as you were to see him at the airport, surprised and not pleased.'

'So you didn't know he was going to be here?' he said, his dark eyes unreadable.

'No, of course I didn't!' she flared. 'I would have told you if I had. I may be far from perfect in your eyes, but no one has ever accused me of being deceitful.' Her voice became calmer. 'I don't see anything wrong in a bit of healthy jealousy. I was jealous of you when I thought that the delightful Jenny meant something to you. I'm jealous of your closeness to Kate, but I don't make a meal of it. As far as I'm concerned, at this moment you're *here* with *me*.'

He gave a low laugh and she thought thankfully that the barrier was coming down.

'You're telling me what you're not,' he said, 'but there's one thing you have to be, and that's blind, if you think there's anything between Kate and me. She's in love with Rowland Ashley, has been for a long time, but he's still got blinkers on. Maybe one day he'll see the treasure that's right under his nose.'

'Kate and Rowland!' she breathed. 'Of course, I should have realised. I always thought we had something in common, a yearning for you, but I was wrong and I'm glad. But Kate and I *do* still have a bond; we're both in love with men that we're going to have to share with a small boy.'

He was standing with his back to the window, the outline of him etched in darkness against the sun's light, and yet it was as if every inch of him was emblazoned in fire, so great was her longing for him.

The stillness was back in him.

'And can you cope with that?'

'You mean a one-to-one-and-a-half relationship?'

she said, recklessly endangering the peace that had
been about to return to them. 'That's for *you* to judge,
Zac.' And she slammed the door shut between the
rooms and flung herself on to the bed.

CHAPTER NINE

CANDACE lay staring miserably at the ceiling, angry with both herself and Zac. Why on earth had she given him cause to think she resented Marcus? Perhaps it was because she wanted to hurt him as he kept hurting her, hit him in his most vulnerable spot. Whatever the reason, she wished she hadn't said it. Yet surely he knew how she felt about Marcus? Hadn't she been chauffeuring him to and fro every Sunday for the last few weeks? And it certainly hadn't been a case of using the boy to get to the man.

'Damn!'

She beat the pillows with her fists. The weekend had got off to a disastrous start. All her bright hopes had been dashed when she'd seen Roddy at the airport. She had known that Zac wouldn't be too pleased about it either, and that he wouldn't see it as just a coincidence. Hadn't they already had words about him, and all for no reason? Then, on top of that, *she'd* made matters worse by the comment about Marcus.

However, one thing was for certain: any friction between Zac and herself must not be allowed to spoil her uncle's special day. It must be concealed until such a time as they could discuss their differences once and for all, because she didn't think she could stand much more.

She got up off the bed at last, and, removing her clothes, stood naked before showering. Would she and Zac ever sleep together? she wondered. Knowing him, it would be only with a wedding-ring on her finger, and the chances of that no sooner looked promising than they disappeared.

For their first meal at the Villa Camille she chose to wear a dress of heavy turquoise cotton with a full skirt, low-cut neckline and three-quarter sleeves, and with it a coral necklace and matching earrings. She had twisted her hair into a long thick plait and let it hang over the front of her shoulder.

Candace knew that she looked good, but she didn't feel it. When she went on to the landing Zac was coming out of his room at the same time and he gave her a cool nod. He was looking good, too, in a white short-sleeved shirt and black trousers. He also looked cool and controlled, showing no signs of their earlier skirmish, and she couldn't help thinking that there were many sides to him, and the one that appealed to her most was the one that he showed his patients. . .and Marcus. There was a deep well of tenderness in him for those in need. What a pity she didn't qualify. He didn't understand her needs; every-body else's except hers.

He had obviously been thinking along the same lines as herself because as their eyes met he said, 'I suggest we do nothing to spoil this time for your uncle and Margot. I would never forgive myself, having been welcomed into his home, if we were responsible for its being any less than enchanted for them.'

For some reason his consideration didn't impress her. It made anger rise again.

'I don't need anyone to tell me that!' she said tartly. 'I love that man. He's the only family I've known since I was twelve. I would never do anything to hurt him. So, my darling Zachary, I'll put on a show if you will.' And as a gong sounded from down below, and the doors of the other rooms began to open, she pulled his head down to hers and kissed him lingeringly.

It would have been hard to say who sparkled the most during the meal, but one thing was for sure, it wasn't Roddy. He was eyeing them both warily as if he couldn't quite decide how close they were, and as Zac regaled them with amusing incidents from Montrose, and Candace laughed light-heartedly while toasting them with several glasses of wine, he looked on morosely.

When they had finished eating, they went into the garden for coffee. It was cooler out there and a big yellow moon hung over the sea, and as Zac strolled among the orange trees with Harry and Margot, Candace found Roddy by her side.

'How do *you* come to be invited to the wedding?' she hissed angrily.

He smiled, pleased to discover that she wasn't as carefree as she had been making out.

'I told you that I'd started working for the old man, didn't I?' he said in a low voice. 'And what line are we in? Wines, of course, which means I come to Portugal frequently. You remember, that's how I found out that your uncle had succumbed to feminine charm at last. I called at the hospital to see you early this morning and was told you'd gone to Portugal. I knew it must be to see Harry, and I suddenly found that I had important business in this part of the world. I managed to get a mid-morning flight, not realising that you weren't travelling until the afternoon, and got here before you. It was then I found out about the wedding and wangled myself an invitation.'

Candace glared at him.

'But why? You're not interested in being at my uncle's wedding.'

'Come on, Candace,' he wheedled. 'We both know that. I'm here because of you.'

'Well, you needn't be!' she snapped. 'I told you the last time I saw you that I wasn't interested.'

'Why? Because of the dashing doctor?'

'Mind your own business, Roddy!' she exploded, and, rising from her seat, went to join the others.

It was a pleasant relaxed evening on the surface. Harry regaled them with the story of how he'd flown to Portugal to rectify his youthful mistake as soon as he'd heard that Margot had been widowed some months previously.

'I'd messed it up once,' he told them. 'I couldn't risk losing her again, and guess what, when I got here, Margot felt the same, and that is why we are going to Faro tomorrow to make our vows.'

'And afterwards?' Candace asked.

'We're going to Madeira. You folks must treat this place as your own. The maids will be on hand to see to your requirememnts. That goes for you too, Roddy. Stay as long as you like,' he said generously. 'The other wedding guests—that's Carlos, Margot's stepson, and the Rodrigues family—will be at the wedding and the meal afterwards, but they will return to their own homes.'

So it was going to be just the heavenly trio, Candace thought grimly, with Zac keeping her at arm's length, and she keeping Roddy at a distance. It promised to be hilarious once the happy couple had left, and as they retired to their rooms for the night she longed for everything to be right between Zac and herself.

It was hot and airless in spite of the fans in the room, and by one o'clock Candace had given up trying to sleep, and so she slipped on the dress that she had worn earlier, and in bare feet tiptoed out into the garden.

She could hear the lapping of the sea out across the sand, and, feeling restless and on edge, she headed for the beach. People were still strolling among the gardens of a large hotel at the water's edge, and a gang of local youths on motorcycles whizzed past along the coast road, the whine of their engines echoing long after they'd gone, but the beach was deserted. A strip of silver sand all to herself.

As she walked along, her footprints indented on its smooth dampness, Candace saw that every so far there were large flat stones, and she was about to step on one of them when Zac's voice came urgently from behind.

'Don't! Don't step on it, Candace!' he cried as he strode towards her. 'That's a Portuguese man-of-war.

She shrank back, shuddering.

'You mean one of those huge stinging jellyfish?'

'Yes, I do. They can be very nasty,' he said tonelessly.

She was recovering.

'What are you doing here? Were you following me?'

'Yes, I was. I saw you leave the house. Are you out of your mind coming down here alone? There are gangs of youths hanging about on the road there and God knows what else.'

'I came out for some air, that's all,' she protested. 'I couldn't sleep, and presume it must have been the same for you.'

'I can sleep at any time and in any conditions if I choose to,' he said in the tone of voice one used to a fractious child. 'Tonight I decided not to.'

'I see. What had you in mind, then? Reading a

medical journal? Or had you decided to stay awake to keep an eye on *my* activities?'

'I'm presuming that you're referring to Carstairs and yourself,' he said evenly, 'and if that is so, the answer is no, I hadn't. You've told me he means nothing to you and I believe you, although it's plain to see that he has other ideas, judging from the way he's continually ogling you. As a matter of fact, I was sitting by my window thinking about life in general when I saw you leave the house.'

She still felt prickly and on edge.

'And did you come to any profound conclusions?'

He gave a low laugh, and she could see the whiteness of his teeth in the moonlight.

'Not then, but I've come to one since. I've decided that a man alone with a beautiful woman on a deserted beach would be a fool not to enjoy the moment, and that's what I intend to do. Come here, Candace,' he said softly, holding out his arms, and like someone mesmerised she went into them.

There was no doubt about who was kissing whom this time. His lips were reminding her that, whatever their differences, the flame between them still burnt strong. His arms holding her close to the hardness of him were the bonds that she would never want to break, and as they clung to each other his lips left her mouth to trace the soft line of her throat and the rising columns of her breasts in the low-cut dress. Then they were lying on the sand beneath the same yellow moon, the sweet desire in them clamouring for fulfilment, but Zac was still Zac. She knew it the moment he rolled away from her and gave a low groan. As she lay quivering he held out his hand and pulled her gently to her feet.

'Let's go back,' he said huskily. 'I, of all people, don't want to be responsible for an unwanted child.'

Tears glittered on her lashes. He was talking as if they were involved in something sleazy. The word screamed inside her head. . .'unwanted'. To carry Zac's child would be the most wanted thing she could ever hope for, and as she searched his face, calm once more in the moonlight, she thought that this would have to stop before she lost her sanity.

The small church where Harry and Margot Garcia were married was old and dark, its gloom lightened only by candles on the altar, and the sun's light splintering the shadows in rainbow shafts through windows of coloured glass.

The bride wore a calf-length dress of cream brocade, with a coronet of yellow roses holding in place a veil of fine lace, while the bridegroom was resplendent in a suit of silver-grey.

Two small girls had preceded her up the aisle, scattering flower petals out of silver baskets, and a young priest, who Candace was surprised to find spoke English, had been waiting for them beside the altar. And now it was over and the wedding party had gathered outside the church.

Carlos Garcia, Margot's stepson, a plump, pleasant Portuguese man, who was shortly to be married himself, was directing them to the wedding cars, and as she and Zac, along with the ever-present Roddy, followed Margot's friends the Rodrigueses to the waiting limousines, Candace was thinking that it was the first time she had seen Zac in a suit, and the effect was something she wasn't likely to forget. It was dark and more formal than her uncle's, and with a white shirt and a silk tie he presented the picture of a very desirable man, and a perfect foil for her own smart dress and jacket of fine pink wool. She knew they made a striking couple. . . outwardly, but it didn't stop her from wondering if there would ever come a day when Harry Carson would come to England especially for *her* wedding.

Roddy, looking somewhat crumpled, was wearing the suit he had worn the previous day, and he had told Candace sheepishly that he hadn't stopped to pack, so consequently the only suit he had with him was the one he had on.

It served him right if he looked limp and creased, she thought. He shouldn't have been in such a hurry to poke his nose into her affairs.

However, crumpled though he might be, she noticed that the suit wasn't having any effect on his ego. The moment that Zac had left her side to try to coax a smile out of the little Rodrigues girl, he was there, wanting to know when he could see her alone.

'You're nothing if not persistent,' she told him coldly. 'It might have escaped your notice, but I came here with Zachary Stephens.'

'It doesn't mean that you're tied to his coat-tails, does it?' he said persuasively. 'And in any case he's not falling over himself to give you his attention by the looks of it.'

'Go away, Roddy,' she hissed. 'Go and play with a Portuguese man-of-war.'

'Eh? What's that?'

'A stinging jellyfish,' she told him sweetly, 'and its sting will be nothing compared to mine if you don't stop pestering me.'

There had been cool pleasantness between Zac and herself during breakfast and in the time that they had lazed by the pool before leaving for the church, and she'd thought that, although it wasn't the most satisfying state of affairs, it was certainly less exhausting than the usual see-saw of their relationship. Those moments on the beach had been an example of that. They had been at outs with each other, and yet she had gone into his arms like a ship into harbour because of her need of him, and it had been the same for Zac. So why couldn't they get the rest of it right? she thought achingly as the wedding cars sped past the Bishop's Palace in its quiet square, and down a narrow street to a large hotel by the harbour.

A table had been set for them in a small room overlooking the sea, and as they ate the delicious food provided by attentive staff, and toasted the bride and groom, Candace felt tears sting as she observed her uncle's happiness.

She had never known that his single state was because he'd loved only one woman, and she wondered bleakly if the same fate was in store for her. Because if she and Zac didn't get together there would be no other man for her. . .ever.

He was teasing the little Rodrigues girl at the other side of the table and she thought, surely he saw that no one could live without touching the lives of others? To be afraid to give of oneself was like being afraid to live, and in a moment of supreme clarity, among the noise and chatter of the wedding party, she accepted that it was not for her to point that out to him. It was something he had to decide for himself, and until he was ready to let her into his life, if ever, she was going to stay away from him. The scars that he bore, still only partly healed, would knit together in the security of her love. . .if he would give her the chance, but there was no way she was going to get down on her knees and beg, and, that being so, the moment they had waved goodbye to Harry and Margo she was going home. He and Roddy could have the pleasure of each other's company.

When her uncle and his new wife had gone silence settled on the villa. Zac had gone to his room and reappeared in swimming trunks, with sunglasses in his hand and a towel over his shoulder.

'I'm going to the beach,' he stated briefly. 'Are you coming?'

'No, I'm going to have a shower,' she said smoothly. 'I'll see you at dinner.'

'Fair enough,' he agreed unsmilingly, and as she watched him stride away towards the sea Candace knew that she wouldn't be seeing him at dinner, not if there was a vacant seat on a flight to northern England.

When she rang Faro airport there were seats available on a Manchester flight in two hours' time, and, after reserving one of them, she rang for a car to take her to the airport, and then began to pack with all speed.

There was no sign of Roddy, and the maids were in their quarters as she left the villa, and as the driver of the hire car turned on to the coast road Candace slithered down in her seat. The last thing she wanted was for Zac to witness her departure.

She'd no need to feel guilty, she assured herself as she checked in at the flight desk. She wasn't doing anything wrong, though she supposed it was a breach of manners to take Zac to Portugal as her guest and leave him there. And if it was, she had her reasons. Maybe it would make him realise that she wasn't forever at his beck and call, and yet, having made such a stand, why did she feel so utterly miserable?

The aircraft was almost full when she boarded. There was just one vacant seat across from her own, and as she reached up to put her flight bag on the shelf above her head Candace saw Roddy making his way down the plane towards her.

She slumped down in her seat in dismayed disbelief. What was *he* doing here? It couldn't have been planned as his amazement was as great as her own when he saw her, but there was pleasure on his part.

'What's going on?' he asked. 'Where's Stephens? I thought you were staying in Monte Gordo until Monday.'

'I decided to get an earlier flight, that's all,' she told him uncomfortably, 'and obviously Zac preferred to stay.' She wasn't going to tell him that he hadn't actually been offered a choice.

'Same here,' he said. 'There didn't seem to be anything to stay for as you were so wrapped up in him. I just managed to get the last seat. . .and I'm glad I did.'

The glint was back in his eye and Candace turned her head away

'Don't be,' she told him. 'I intend to pass the time reading and sleeping, and when we land at the other end I'm going straight home. . .alone. Understood?'

'OK,' he said dejectedly. 'I think I understood from the moment I saw you with that guy.'

All through Sunday Candace was on edge. She kept thinking guiltily of Marcus with no visitors. Should she go to see him? No, not without Zac. It would make matters worse when they met again if he found out that she'd been to see the boy while he had been left high and dry in Portugal.

On Monday morning she found herself jumping at every sound, expecting Zac to come banging on her door demanding an explanation. In the end she went into the town and wandered aimlessly around the shops. She had booked the day off as a holiday and it had to be got through somehow. When evening came she turned the TV up so that she wouldn't hear the bell, and then turned it down again, feeling that her behaviour was bordering on childish, but she needn't have worried, it never rang.

Kate's first words on the ward on Tuesday morning were,

'And how did you folks enjoy your weekend in Portugal?'

Candace was about to answer when Zac's voice spoke from behind and she froze.

'It was interesting, Kate. . .and very illuminating,' he said drily. 'I've heard it said that you can't beat going on holiday with a person if you really want to get to know them.'

Kate was eyeing them both warily.

'Er. . .I see. . .or do I?' she said awkwardly. 'In that case, I'll leave you to reminisce,' and she bustled off.

'That was a charming trick you pulled,' Zac said furiously when they were alone, 'sneaking off with Carstairs. I don't know why I ever believe a word you say. You invite me to spend the weekend with you and then disappear. You have *some* nerve, Candace!'

She faced him squarely. He was right, of course, but then *he* wasn't exactly blameless, was he?

'When did you get back?' she asked calmly.

'Yesterday as planned,' he answered coldly. 'Why, did you expect me to come running after you?'

'No. I didn't, and I don't know why I'm explaining, but with regard to Roddy, yes, he *was* on my flight, but not with my knowledge. It had nothing to do with me. He'd decided to go home because he wasn't getting anywhere with me. That's the truth, take it or leave it, and I'm not particularly bothered what you do, because from now on I'm going to get on with my own life, and I've decided it will be a lot less painful if I do it alone.'

Zac's eyes were hard as agate.

'No wonder I was wary of making a commitment to you,' he gritted.

That was the last straw.

'Don't blame me for that,' she flared. 'The fault wasn't on my part, though you persuaded yourself that it was. You needed somebody to take your past frustrations out on, and I happened to come along. Well, not any more, Zac.' Her voice thickened with treacherous tears. 'Not any more.'

Having made the big decision, Candace found it wasn't easy to keep to it, not when the man in question was everywhere she went. She supposed it was only to be expected, as they *did* work together, but had it been like that before, with Zac forever on her heels, in Theatre, Outpatients, Neonatal, the labour ward, and always with his eyes guarded, his mouth unsmiling?

On the Friday after the disastrous weekend in Portugal, Candace had just observed that one of the patients in the labour ward was losing Meconium, a tar-like substance, from the birth canal. At the same second Zac came striding in. He paused by the bed and on seeing what was occurring said briefly, 'You realise that's Meconium?'

'Yes, I do,' she told him with equal restraint, 'but. . .'

'But nothing,' he said abruptly. 'There is obviously foetal distress. . .Nurse. I would have expected you to be aware of that.'

Candace stared at him. He had made the comment without having examined the young mother-to-be, and Zac knew as well as anybody, probably more so, that the seriousness of Meconium from the birth canal depended on the position of the baby, and this one

wasn't in the vertex position. . .it was a breech, which
indicated there was no cause for immediate alarm.

'The baby is in the breech position. . .Doctor,' she
said levelly.

He was staring at her with an intensity that brought
swift colour to her cheeks.

'Huh? What?' he asked absently, and she thought
that his mind must be in some far off place. . .Portugal
maybe, if the grimness of his expression was anything
to go by.

'It's in the breech position,' she repeated patiently.

Suddenly he was back on the same planet, and it was
Zac's colour that was deepening now.

'A breech? Oh, yes, of course. She's one of Ashley's
patients, isn't she?'

'Yes,' she told him, still amazed at his vagueness. He
looked tired and out of sorts, but it was unheard of for
Zac to get muddled about a patient.

'Carry on, then,' he instructed. 'No problem.'

No problem for the patient, she thought, except that
the baby wasn't in the best of positions, but what about
the doctor? There seemed to be a problem there, and
as if aware that she was making a silent diagnosis on
him as they moved away from the bed he said stiffly, 'I
shall be seeing Marcus this weekend. Any messages?'

That hurt. She had been relegated to the sidelines,
but it was only to be expected, she supposed. He wasn't
asking if *she* wanted to see the boy too, just a curt
question. . .had she any message for him?

'No,' she told him. 'Marcus is too young and vulnerable to understand the workings of *our* minds. I don't
want to hurt or confuse him.'

'But you don't mind hurting or confusing me?' he
said harshly.

'Yours is self-inflicted,' she told him as futile anger

began to spark inside her, and as Rowland Ashley
appeared to examine his patient she left Zac, and went
to join the senior obstetrician.

There was no triumph in her as she thought about
Zac's absent-mindedness later in the day. He'd been
ill, hadn't he? And perhaps not got the benefit he
might have done from his weekend in the sun, she
thought guiltily. Yet those things wouldn't put him off
his stride. He was too strong and determined for that.
Pity he hadn't been the same in his pursuit of herself,
she decided, as she ate her solitary evening meal and
contemplated the empty weekend ahead.

Kate called round on Saturday morning, and when
Candace saw her standing on the doorstep her spirits
lifted. She liked Kate Summers, liked her a lot, and, as
she had told Zac in that moment of painful clarity, they
had a bond. . .they both loved a man with a child.

'I love this apartment,' Kate said as Candace was
making coffee. 'The blues and yellows are so pretty,
and such an unusual combination.'

Candace smiled.

'It suits me for now.'

'That doesn't sound very permanent,' Kate
observed.

'Possibly not,' she agreed cautiously, 'but life
changes all the time.'

'Yes, it does,' Kate admitted, 'and might I be nosy
and ask what's changed between Zac and yourself? I
thought we were going to have a big romance on the
unit.'

'What about yourself?' Candace fenced, and then
felt ashamed at betraying Zac's confidence, but she
needn't have worried, Kate was smiling.

'You mean with Rowland? It's progressing. . .
slowly. . .but I can afford to wait. He's had a bad time,

and even though his wife didn't deserve him, he's entitled to his grief. He'll be ready for me one day, and I'll be there,' she said serenely, 'but I came to talk about you and Zac, not me.'

Candace swallowed. She badly needed to talk to someone.

'Have you got time to listen?' she asked.

'All the time in the world,' Kate replied, and so she told her, right from the beginning about Camilla, and how Zac had been there then, and how she had been dumbfounded to find him still at Montrose.

'So you know him from way back!' Kate said in surprise. 'I didn't know that. I guessed that you'd met before somewhere, but had no idea it was so long ago and in what circumstances. And did you fall in love with him then?'

'No, I hated him, or thought I did. He was always putting me down—still is, in fact. He calls me the poor little rich nurse. Thinks, or perhaps I should say thought, I was useless.'

'He has to have changed his mind about that!' Kate cried. 'You're one of my best nurses.'

'I think he has, up to a point,' Candace told her, 'but because he had a pretty grim childhood he's wary of someone like me, and basically that's the root of the trouble. I love him desperately, and I think he knows it, but on his part there's an unwillingness to accept me as I am.'

Kate tutted.

'I love that man dearly, in a purely platonic sense. He has honour and integrity, and a dedication that is somewhat rare these days, but he must be blind if he can't see what a lovely girl you are.'

Candace gave a sad little laugh.

'That's what he said *I* was when I thought he was in love with you. . .blind.'

'And he put you right, I take it?'

'Yes, but he does have a very high regard for you.'

'As I say, it's mutual,' Kate replied, 'but it's his regard for you that's under discussion. I've seen the way he looks at you with his heart in his eyes.'

'Then it must be a stony gaze,' she said, 'because his heart *is* a stone.'

'I don't think so,' Kate said gently, 'but, whatever it is, I came here because I thought you should know that he's thinking of leaving Montrose.'

Candace felt the colour draining from her face.

'Are you sure?'

'Yes. He's been headhunted. Got the proposition only today, and I think he'll accept the offer.'

'Is it in the Derbyshire area?' Candace asked slowly.

'Yes, it is! How did you guess?' and then in answer to her own question, 'The boy, of course. . .Marcus.'

'Zac is considering fostering or possibly adoption,' Candace told her.

'It takes some man to do something like that,' Kate said thoughtfully, 'but the boy will need a mother, too.'

'Yes, I know,' Candace said bleakly, and with a token show of defiance, 'and, that being so, Zac will have to find him one, and I hope she does better in the suitability stakes than I did.'

'So there's no chance of you getting back together?'

'I don't think so, Kate, but thanks for trying.'

'I could shake Zachary Stephens,' Kate said as she got up to go. 'It's as we've said before. . .why are the men in our lives so complicated?'

'Why indeed?' Candace echoed, as the thought of not seeing Zac again tore at her heart. Why indeed?

CHAPTER TEN

WHEN Kate had gone Candace sat staring into space. If the weekend had promised to be empty before, now it loomed like a black abyss. So Zac had taken her at her word. He was getting his priorities right. . .moving to be near Marcus. . .and away from *her*.

'And is it surprising?' she asked herself as she saw her wan face in the mirror. 'Your friendship with him was a non-starter before it even got off the ground.' God only knew it could hardly be called an affair. A few moments of passion, and the rest had been uncertainty and misunderstanding.

As she went to her bedroom at a far earlier hour than usual it was with the hope inside her that maybe Kate had been wrong. Perhaps he would refuse the offer, but even as she dared to indulge in optimism Candace knew he wouldn't do that. Zac had nothing to keep him at Montrose, and everything to attract him to Derbyshire.

She wasn't competing against another woman for the man she loved. She had two opponents. One was an endearing small boy, and the other, a nameless woman from long ago who had abandoned her child and scarred him for ever. There was no way she could fight Marcus because *she* loved him too, and Zac's hurt was too deep in his soul for her to break through his distrust.

Candace went to the bedroom window and stood looking out into the summer dusk. In the distance the hospital building was outlined against the sky, its many windows ablaze with light, its heartbeat just as strong at night as in the daytime, and Candace thought that wherever she went, whatever she did, Montrose would aways be labelled in her mind as the place where sorrow came easily, and happiness was hard to find.

'How was Marcus?' she asked Zac when they came face to face in the corridor on Monday morning.

'Fine,' he said with clipped politeness. 'I took him to the cinema and then for a meal in one of the fast-food places.'

'I imagine he enjoyed that,' she commented in a similar tone.

'Yes, I think he did. . .up to a point.'

She was turning to go, determined that he wasn't going to get the idea that she was using Marcus as a talking point.

'He had a message for you.'

She swivelled back to face him.

'Oh! What was it?'

'He said to tell you that he had a fight with one of the short-stay kids who said his mum was nicer than you.'

Her eyes were tender.

'And who won?'

'Who do you think?' he said with a twisted smile, and went on his way.

Candace stared after him. She was desperate to know if he *was* leaving, but there was no way she was going to ask him outright. It would have to be a case of relying on the hospital grapevine and it rarely failed.

In this instance, it came up with the answer that very morning in the shape of Debbie, who hadn't got a sharp little nose for nothing.

'Zac Stephens is leaving,' she said as they assisted with the routine delivery of a lusty baby boy.

Candace felt her heart clench with dismay. So there was to be no reprieve.

'When is he going?' she asked, striving to sound only mildly interested.

'In three weeks, at the end of the month. Kate says she'll be collecting for a farewell gift for him. He'll be missed here at Montrose,' she said philosophically, 'but I suppose our loss is someone else's gain.'

'Yes, I'm sure it will be,' Candace agreed faintly, as she wiped mucus from the baby's mouth, and Gordon Grampion clamped the cord in two places and then cut and tied it.

She didn't see Zac to speak to for the rest of the day and in a perverse sort of way she was glad. Debbie had confirmed what Kate had hinted at on Saturday and she needed time to adjust to it.

Would he have made the same decision if she hadn't told him he was out of her life? she asked herself a dozen times during the evening. Had she brought this misery upon herself? Could she have carried on as they were, seesawing from delight to disillusion? The answer was no. She had put the ball in Zac's court, and this was the answer. That conclusion, along with a vision of Marcus with the famous scowl on his face and his small fists bunched, fighting over *her*, took away the last of her composure, and she sat down and wept.

During the days that followed Candace was aware that everyone on the unit seemed to have spoken to Zac about his impending departure except herself. They talked about the job, occasionally in a restrained sort of way they discussed Marcus, and once they had even commented on the weather, but there had been no mention between them of his leaving Montrose, until one day, when Candace was assisting Gordon Grampion, he'd collared Zac as he was passing and said, 'Here, old chap, hold on a minute. I hardly ever seem to see you these days. Keep meaning to ask if you've changed your mind about leaving us. You're going to be missed you know. Isn't he, Nurse?'

Candace had become very still. Her legs felt weak as if they were going to cave in. What was she supposed to say to that? Zac was watching her with a strange expression on his face, and she supposed if she had wanted it, here was the opportunity to convey the message that *she* certainly didn't want him to go, but if she was going to tell him that there was no way she wanted Gordon to be the vehicle for her plea.

'I think that everyone at Montrose will miss Dr Stephens,' she said without raising her head.

'Except yourself, eh, Candace?' Zac said in a low voice as Gordon's attention was momentarily diverted.

Her head came up at that and she looked him squarely in the eye.

'*You* said that, Zac,' she told him coldly, 'not me.'

They were on dangerous ground and she wanted to be off it—no more emotional quagmires for *her*—and so, in spite of an insane longing to throw herself into his arms and beg him to stay, she gave him a cool nod and said, 'And now. . .if you'll excuse me.'

The next Saturday was the hospital's summer fête, a big charity event that staff were asked to support. Candace was glad of it because it would help to fill the weekend. There were two weekends before Zac was due to go, and the next one was also not as empty as it might have been because she had had a phone call from Janet McCready to say that the christening was to be on that Sunday, and would she be available.

She could have told Janet that she had never been more available than she was now, and that she was desperate to fill in the empty hours, but instead she just told her warmly that she certainly was, and asked what time the big event was.

'Two o'clock in the afternoon at St Mark's church,' she said, 'and afterwards we're all going back to our place for a buffet meal.'

'That sounds lovely,' Candace said. 'I'm longing to see the babies again.'

'They're doing fine,' the proud mother said, and when she rang off Candace remembered that she had been going to ask if they had managed to find all the necessary godparents.

The Friends of Montrose Hospital were organising the fête, and when Candace, along with the rest of the staff on the maternity unit, offered her services, she was put in charge of the children's play area, where swings, trampolines, rope ladders, climbing frames and various other amusements were to be erected. A daunting prospect!

There was a large marquee where afternoon teas were to be served, various sideshows, donkey rides, and an assortment of stalls. . .and the children's playground which had been fenced off, with a small admission fee gaining entrance to the whole.

She had expected it to be an exhausting job and it was: watching that none of her young charges strayed or got hurt among the hilarity, while their parents were able to stroll around the fête in comfort; and at the same time dispensing plasters and antiseptic cream for minor scratches from the first-aid box that the hospital had provided.

By the middle of the afternoon Candace was feeling hot and sticky, and the tea-tent beckoned invitingly, but until someone came to relieve her she would have to stay put.

There had been no sign of Zac among the crowds, and she knew that he hadn't allowed himself to become embroiled in any of the activities, which brought her to the conclusion that he had either gone to Avonlea to see Marcus, or, being on the point of severing his ties with Montrose, had decided to stay away.

That had been until a small voice said at her elbow, 'Hello, Candace,' and she swung round to find Marcus looking up at her with Zac beside him.

In the joy of the moment, the sense of loss and futility that always seemed to be there was banished, and she picked him up and hugged him to her.

'What a lovely surprise,' she said laughingly, and as her eyes met Zac's she felt he must surely have known that she wasn't just referring to Marcus.

As she put him down on to his feet again he said eagerly, 'Can I go on all the things, Candace?'

'Of course you can,' she told him. 'Give me your jacket so you won't get too warm.'

'How much is it?' Zac asked, fishing in his pocket for small change.

'My treat,' she said, and they exchanged a smile as the memory of Marcus saying the same words when he'd bought them all a cornet came to mind.

He was already running towards the trampolines and Zac said awkwardly, 'I suppose I'd better stay with him to keep an eye on him.'

'Yes, do,' she agreed fervently. 'It's not the easiest

thing in the world watching children in an area like
this.'

Candace wanted him to go so she could calm down.
She was dithering like a dewy-eyed schoolgirl because
the man she loved had appeared, but as she sank down
on to the grass for a moment's respite there was a cry of
alarm. She looked up and saw a toddler who had been
left unattended and had wandered into the play park,
running with incredible speed on its tiny legs towards
the fast moving wooden swing-boats. Quite unaware of
any danger, the little one was dashing straight into the
path of one of them, and as the two bigger children
seated one at each end shouted their enjoyment,
oblivious to what was happening below, Candace was
on her feet and moving with the speed of light.

As she flew across the grass she could hear Zac's feet
pounding behind her, but she got there first, and as she
flung the child out of the way, the swing-boat hit her
on the shoulder.

It wasn't a head-on blow, but the impact of it
knocked her off her feet, and as the toddler ran off,
screaming for its mother, Candace lay there with closed
eyes, weak with relief. . .and the pain that was rocketing along her neck and arm.

'Candace! My God! You could have been killed!
You should have let me. . .' Zac was gasping as he
bent over her, his face bleached with shock. Candace
was drifting off into blankness and she knew she must
be in a bad way, because she was imagining there were
tears in his eyes.

Her lapse into unconsciousness must have been only
a matter of seconds for when she surfaced again she
was still on the grass and Marcus was by her side
breaking his heart.

'She's dead, Zac,' he was howling, and Zac, who was

gently feeling her arm and shoulder, was assuring him
raggedly,

'No, she isn't, Marcus. Candace *isn't* dead. She was
knocked out for a moment. Now calm down. It won't
make her feel any better if she sees you all upset.'

Candace opened her eyes at that and said weakly,
'I'm all right, Marcus, don't worry, darling. It was an
accident, and. . .'

'Shush, Candace,' Zac interrupted. 'The St John
people are bringing a stretcher. I don't want you
walking after a blow like that, and I suppose you'd
object if I carried you.'

Her eyes closed again. She wouldn't object at all; it
might make the pain she was in more bearable if Zac
held her in his arms.

'How badly does it hurt?' he asked, and there was
anger in his voice. 'I shall have something to say to the
organisers of this lot, lumbering you with the play-park
all on your own.'

'It's more bearable now,' she said in a stronger voice,
intent on reassuring Marcus, who was rubbing his eyes
with a grimy hand as his sobs subsided.

'And so what's going on here?' a cheerful voice
asked as two St John Ambulance men put down the
stretcher they had been carrying.

Zac explained what had happened and the same man
said, 'Well, it couldn't have happened in a better place,
even though most of the hospital folk *are* at the fête.'

'Yes, but Casualty will be ticking over as usual,' Zac
said tersely. 'Head for there, and the boy and I will
follow, and watch the lady's left side—that's where she
took the blow.'

'Leave it to us, sonny boy,' he said, and Zac looked
as if he could have throttled him.

'I'm a doctor. . .from this hospital,' he barked, 'not

sonny boy, and this lady is a nurse. I shall be taking over once we get inside.'

'OK, Doc,' the man said, unperturbed. 'I get the message, but you can't blame me for thinking you were a family out for the day.'

As they lifted her on to the stretcher, Candace couldn't help thinking that she wished they were a family, instead of three separate units: a stubborn man, a frustrated woman, and a vulnerable small boy.

X-rays showed that there were no bones broken, just severe bruising, and a jarring of the neck for which she was provided with a collar. The doctor in Casualty decreed that she must stay in overnight as a precaution, and as Zac was in agreement with the decision, and Marcus was back to his old self now she wasn't dead, Candace accepted it with good grace.

The fête was over by this time, and when she had been allocated a bed in Women's Surgical the nurse said, 'Zac Stephens and the little boy are still here. Do you feel up to visitors?'

Candace smiled. She felt a wreck, probably looked one too, and the sedative she had been given was beginning to take effect, but she wasn't going to sleep until she'd seen them. . .until she knew they were all right.

As the man and boy walked down the ward towards her, Candace thought there was something forlorn about them, though she didn't know why. Zac was moving with his usual decisive stride, and Marcus, though obviously tired, was skipping along by his side. Perhaps it was the absence of a woman's company, she thought, and knew that only Zac could remedy that.

When they reached her bed, Marcus commandeered the only available chair and Zac stood looking down on her. There was concern in his eyes, and the gnawing anxiety she'd seen many times in the eyes of those visiting a loved one, but *she* wasn't that, was she? Not in the true sense of the word. Because she was nervous, unsure how to approach him, she decided to be cautious, and knew it to be the right attitude when he said abruptly, 'How are you?'

'Sore,' she replied in like manner, and longed for those tender moments in the play-park to return.

'I've just torn a strip off the lady chairman of the Friends committee,' he said grimly. 'I asked her how many pairs of eyes you were expected to have doing a job like that.'

'You didn't have to,' she protested. 'The blame for the accident lies at the door of a careless parent. It wasn't connected with any of the children I was overseeing.'

He was not to be appeased.

'The fact remains that they shouldn't expect one person to be responsible for all those children.'

Candace closed her eyes. Was his concern for herself or about the effects of poor administration?

'We'll go. You're tired,' he said, and looking down at the boy, 'And so is this young man. I'll have to take him home, I'm afraid, as my flat is only big enough to accommodate me,' he said apologetically. 'Will you be all right?'

'Yes, of course,' she told him drowsily. 'I can look after myself. See to Marcus.'

'Zachary Stephens left a message for you last night,' one of the nurses said as Candace struggled into sluggish wakefulness the following morning. 'He said that you were falling asleep while he was talking to you and wouldn't have heard what he was saying.'

'And what was that?'

'He told us to tell you that he's being shown around his new hospital today. The appointment was made some time ago and he can't very well cancel it. He stressed that you weren't to go home unless you were sure you could cope, and he would see you at the first opportunity.'

'I can cope,' she said firmly as loneliness swamped her again, and to prove it she eased herself out of the borrowed hospital nightdress and began to get dressed, the fact that she was sore and aching not being allowed to deter her.

That night she was in bed by half-past seven, aware that another day in Montrose would have been the wisest thing, but there was nothing worse than being in hospital with no visitors, and she could hardly expect Zac to be at her beck and call in his last days at Montrose.

Monday morning brought with it less pain and the decision to go in work. She could have used the accident as an excuse to miss Zac's final days. It would be less harrowing, but as he was still bent on going out of her life every moment she might spend with him was precious.

He came up behind her as she was getting out of her car and said tetchily, 'What are you doing here?'

Candace stiffened. No solicitude, no praise for making the attempt, just an irritable question, and on that score she wouldn't have admitted it if she had been dropping in her tracks.

'I'm much better, otherwise I wouldn't be here,' she said coolly.

'I called at your place last night, but got no answer,' he said in a tone that was a mixture of concern and accusation.

'That would be because I was in bed by half-past seven,' she explained with sweet reasonableness.

His brow cleared.

'I see, and so as you are assuring me that you're fit and well, can I ask a favour?'

She tensed. This was something unheard of!

'Yes, go ahead.'

'The weekend coming will be my last at Montrose. As you may be aware, I finish the following Friday.'

Oh, she was aware all right!

'And I wondered if you would be free to view a property with me. After all, I'm going to have to find somewhere to live, and I'm sick of hospital accommodation. I've never had a home in the true sense of the word, and feel that now is the time to remedy that. It occurred to me that another opinion would be helpful. The house is in a small village in Derbyshire. I saw it yesterday and liked it.'

'This is for yourself. . .and Marcus, I take it?' she said carefully.

'Er. . .yes. I'm going to instigate the proper proceedings for adoption in the near future.'

Candace was hanging on to the car door as if it were a life support machine. 'Yes, certainly I'll come,' she offered, and wondered why she had never noticed before that she had masochistic tendencies.

'This coming Saturday then. I'll pick you up around lunchtime.'

'Yes, whatever,' she agreed absently as the nerve of his request began to register. The next thing she knew, he would be asking her to help him choose fixtures and fittings!

'I wouldn't have been able to go with you if it had been the Sunday,' she told him. 'That's the day of the McCready christenings.'

'Ah, yes,' he murmured, 'when the little Camilla will be given a pretty name. . .and a godmother.'

'Not just a god*mother*, I would hope.'

He shrugged. 'It's whatever suits *them*, I suppose.' And the subject was dropped.

As the days went by Candace kept thinking of the weekend ahead. She was to be involved in two new beginnings, but neither of them really concerned herself.

On the Saturday she had been asked to pass an opinion on the house that Zac was planning to live in for his new life with Marcus, and on the Sunday she was to take part in the christening of three little girls on the threshold of *their* lives. On both occasions she would be there merely in the role of onlooker, and it was a depressing thought. Would *she* ever have the chance to move into a new house with someone she loved, she asked herself, or give a christening party for a child that belonged to *her*?

It proved to be a fraught week on the unit, with every bed occupied, and Kate commenting that it looked as if every pregnant mother in the area had decided to have her baby at the same time.

Two healthy sets of twins were delivered, all boys, along with various other normal births, but they were offset by the usual traumas. A baby girl born some days previously and still in Neonatal because of low birth weight and slow feeding problems had shown abnormalities when the neonatal screening test was carried out on a blood sample. Further tests showed that pituitary and thyroid malfunction had occurred during the pregnancy, a situation that could not be rectified by transfer of the mother's thyroxine.

The anxious parents were told that daily doses of

thyroxine would have to commence immediately to combat the risk of brain damage, and Zac explained that, when their child was discharged from the hospital, it would need continuing paediatric care.

Added to that, there was a stillbirth. The baby of a Cypriot woman, who, along with her husband, had just opened a restaurant in the town, was born dead for no apparent reason. In her late thirties, the mother had only recently arrived in England, and so consequently the pregnancy had not been monitored at Montrose.

During the last weeks of gestation she *had* been seen by Rowland Ashley, and no cause for concern had been evident, but the fact remained that the baby did not breathe at birth, and no amount of resuscitation made any difference.

The mother's grief could be heard all over the unit as she wailed over the dead infant in her arms, and the father, standing ashen-faced beside her, was just as distressed. As Zac went in to talk to them, Candace and the rest of the staff knew that the sorrow they were experiencing was unique in its futility.

The birth would have to be registered, and 'stillborn' shown as the cause of death, and a baptism arranged if only to acknowledge its brief and tragic appearance, but at that precise moment in time such procedures were far from the minds of the parents. Instead of a lusty howling infant they had a baby to bury, and there was no prescription available to take away the pain of that.

The house that Zac was interested in was one of four, and it was new, which surprised Candace. For some reason she had expected an old stone house, and she eyed the small, attractive devlopment with interest.

Zac was watching her carefully.

'Not what you were expecting?' he questioned.

It wasn't, but, given the choice, she knew that she preferred it to an old building. She gave a strained laugh.

'No, it isn't. I imagined you choosing something more atmospheric.'

He shook his head.

'I prefer to create my own atmosphere,' he said with a tight smile. 'I don't want my first home to be full of other folks' vibes. I don't want anybody else's stamp on it.'

'I can understand that,' she said gravely. 'Your past is a ghost that you haven't quite laid yet, isn't it?'

'You understand that, then?'

She sighed. 'Of course I do.'

Zac smiled, his face softening.

'I'm going to put that right in the very near future, Candace. Do you believe me?'

'Yes, I do,' she said quietly. 'Marcus will make all the difference.'

'Marcus? Oh, yes, he will, no doubt about that.'

There was nothing else she could say to that and they continued on their tour of the house. It was roomy and attractive, though much smaller than any house she had lived in prior to taking up nursing, but she felt that she would like to live in it herself. There was a large back garden and at the bottom of it was a copse with a stream running through it. Paradise for a small boy.

'Well?' he asked, when they went outside for a last look at the exterior.

'It's lovely,' she said sincerely. 'I couldn't have chosen better myself,' and if he thought that was a hint, too bad. Had he no idea how painful all this was for her?

'Are you going to call to see Marcus while we're in the neighbourhood?' she asked as they drove home. To her surprise he shook his head.

'No, not today. I'm picking him up tomorrow.'

'Ah, yes, tomorrow it's the christenings,' she said, perking up at the mention of it. 'I've bought Camilla a tiny silver bracelet.'

He gave her a quick sideways glance.

'You're really looking forward to it, aren't you?'

'Of course,' she said simply. 'Being godmother is one function I *can* manage.'

'What's that supposed to mean?' he asked sharply.

'Work it out for yourself, Zac,' she told him, knowing that he didn't have to.

The vestry at St Mark's church was full of babies, parents and godparents. Lillian, and the shortly to be named Victoria, were sleeping, but baby Camilla was exercising her lungs to some extent and Janet handed her to Candace.

'Here, go to your godmother,' she said with a smile. 'Maybe you'll be quiet for her,' and amazingly, the moment Candace cuddled the baby to her, she closed her eyes and, with a tiny pink fist laid against her cheek, she slept.

Lillian's godparents were to be Alex's sister and her husband, Victoria's Janet's brother and his wife, and, as she nursed the baby, Candace was trying to work out who was to partner herself. As if guessing her thoughts, Janet announced with only mild panic, 'Ten minutes to the start of the service and we're a godfather short.'

'Who is he?' Candace asked with only moderate interest. It didn't really matter who he was. He was bound to be a stranger.

'Your question is answered,' Janet said with a relieved laugh. 'Here he is.'

When Candace looked up she saw Zac framed in the doorway with Marcus by his side. Her eyes widened in disbelief. So Janet had asked two of them from the maternity unit to be godparents. Why hadn't he told her?

They both looked scrubbed and clean, Zac in the smart suit he had worn for her uncle's wedding, and Marcus in a white shirt, red tie, and long grey trousers. A picture of a very attractive man and an engaging small boy. Yet there was that aura of incompleteness about them that she had sensed before. Was there a plea in the two pairs of dark eyes fixed on her?

Yet Zac's face was serene as they came across to her, and he said with a whimsical smile, 'You see, you're not the only one doing the honours.'

'So it would seem,' she said drily. 'Why didn't you tell me?'

'I thought it best that it should be a surprise. It might have ruined your anticipation knowing that you were going to be lumbered with *me*.'

'It's certainly a surprise,' she assured him, ignoring the rest of his remarks, and with a smile for Marcus, 'It's a pleasure I hadn't bargained for.'

He grinned back at her, and she saw that a new tooth was appearing in the gap.

The church was full, the service solemn and moving, and as they made their responses as godparents Candace felt tearful. She and Zac seemed to be together in so many ways, she thought—their jobs, their affection for Marcus, this christening, he had even asked her to help him choose a house, but their minds didn't run on the same tracks, did they? And that was the problem.

When they got back to the McCready house, photo-

graphs were taken in the garden, and Candace posed
with Camilla in her arms and Zac and Marcus on either
side.

The food was delicious, but she lacked appetite. She
had been enjoying the occasion until the photograph
was taken. They had looked like a family, mother,
father, small boy, the family that the St John man had
thought they were, but it wasn't ever going to be like
that, was it? Had she given up on Zac too soon? Should
she have stuck it out and hoped that in the end he
would really accept her? No. The decision had to come
from him, otherwise she would never be clear in her
mind as to whether she had cajoled him into a commitment that he didn't really want. And he had made the
choice, hadn't he? He was leaving her behind, and
although she'd had long enough to get used to the idea,
it was still like a knife in her heart.

Zac was chatting to the McCreadys, and Marcus
tucking into the food, when she slipped into the garden
unobserved. Standing beneath a huge apple tree that
was out of sight of the house, Candace thought that
she might as well get a transfer to a London hospital
and make her base the Belgravia house as before.
There was nothing for her here, and in the despair of
the moment she hid her face against the gnarled trunk
of the tree.

'What are you doing out here?' Zac's voice asked
from behind her.

She didn't move. Tears were threatening, shameful
tears she was about to shed over a man who didn't
want her. A man who wanted a family without a wife.

He moved forward and, placing his hands on her
shoulders, eased her round to face him.

'Candace. . .I asked you what you were doing out
here?'

She couldn't be bothered with any more pretence.

'I came out to get away from you. . .and all the pain that goes with you,' she said simply.

A shadow crossed his face, and his grip on her tightened.

'I've been waiting until today to ask you a question,' he said, as the afternoon sun bathed them in its golden glow, and the sounds of the christening party drifted over.

'What is it?' she gulped, fighting for control. Was he going to ask her to choose his curtains for him?

'You once referred to us as a one-to-one-and-a-half relationship,' he said, 'which was true. I'm asking you if that would be enough. Would you take me on those terms?'

The unhappiness in her face was giving way to amazed joy, but the questions were still in her mind.

'I'll take you on any terms, Zac,' she said with quiet dignity, 'on one condition.'

'And what's that?' he asked, looking deep into her eyes.

'That you really want *me*. . .the poor little rich nurse. Candace Carson, who has always irritated you because we come from different worlds.'

'It *is* you I want, Candace,' he said with deadly seriousness. 'I've wanted you ever since I saw you that night at the Christmas ball, and like an idiot I've let past hurts blind my vision, warp my judgement; but not any more. You're never out of my mind; my bones ache for you. I want to be with you the rest of my life, you in my arms, you waiting for me when I come home each day. The house we saw yesterday was for us. . .if you'll have me. I was going to ask you to marry me while we were there, but my nerve failed me. The thought of what would happen if you said no was too

unbearable to contemplate, because I knew if you did
say that I'd have deserved it.'

She reached up and cradled his face in gentle hands.

'I ache for you too, Zac,' she said softly, 'and I'd
resigned myself to being like my uncle. . .on my own,
because the one person I wanted was out of reach, but
now you've brought me into the light again and I can
forget past miseries.

'You say that you're offering me only a one-to-one-
and-a-half relationship because of Marcus, but that
isn't so. I love him as much as you do. The scales of
our life together will be evenly balanced.'

'I don't deserve you,' he said raggedly, as his mouth
sought hers and his arms cradled her gently to him.
When at last they drew apart, he said sombrely, 'I've
been so busy hanging on to the chip on my shoulder
that I hadn't the brains to see I was being offered a
marvellous recompense for the knocks I'd endured, in
the form of a beautiful, desirable woman who was
prepared to take me as I am, though God knows why.'

Candace raised her arms and traced the outline of
his broad shoulders gently.

'There's nothing there now,' she said with a laugh of
pure joy.

'No, and there never will be again,' he promised.

It was a year later, and the heavily pregnant woman
holding a lively small boy by the hand was the last in
the queue to see the doctor. Her turn came eventually,
and as they were ushered into his office he looked up
and asked gravely, 'And how are you this morning,
Mrs Stephens?'

'Just as well and happy as when you left me at
breakfast-time, Doctor,' she said with a smile.

His own smile was tender, and, getting up from

behind his desk, he came round to them. Placing one hand gently on her thickened waistline, he hugged the boy to him with the other, and over his small dark head asked softly, 'And how is the world's second most wanted child this morning?'

Her eyes lingered on the man and the boy, so alike that they could have been father and son, and then she looked down to where his hand lay above their unborn infant, and said serenely, 'She's doing fine, Zachary, my darling, just fine.'

Temptation

Lost Loves

'Right Man...Wrong time'

All women are haunted by a lost love—a disastrous first romance, a brief affair, a marriage that failed.

A second chance with him...could change everything.

Lost Loves, a powerful, sizzling mini-series from Temptation continues in April 1995 with...

**Even Cowboys Get the Blues
by Carin Rafferty**

MILLS & BOON

GET 4 BOOKS
AND A MYSTERY GIFT

FREE

Return the coupon below and we'll send you 4 Love on Call novels absolutely FREE! We'll even pay the postage and packing for you.

We're making you this offer to introduce you to the benefits of Reader Service: FREE home delivery of brand-new Love on Call novels, at least a month before they are available in the shops, FREE gifts and a monthly Newsletter packed with information.

Accepting these FREE books places you under no obligation to buy, you may cancel at any time, even after receiving just your free shipment. Simply complete the coupon below and send it to:

HARLEQUIN MILLS & BOON, **FREEPOST**, PO BOX 70, CROYDON CR9 9EL.

Yes, please send me 4 Love on Call novels and a mystery gift as explained above. Please also reserve a subscription for me. If I decide to subscribe I shall receive 4 superb new titles every month for just £7.20* postage and packing free. I understand that I am under no obligation whatsoever. I may cancel or suspend my subscription at any time simply by writing to you, but the free books and gift will be mine to keep in any case.
I am over 18 years of age.

1EP5D

Ms/Mrs/Miss/Mr _____

Address _____

_____

_____

——————————————— Postcode _____

MILLS & BOON

LOVE ON CALL

The books for enjoyment this month are:

SMOOTH OPERATOR	Christine Adams
RIVALS FOR A SURGEON	Drusilla Douglas
A DAUNTING DIVERSION	Abigail Gordon
AN INDISPENSABLE WOMAN	Margaret Holt

Treats in store!

Watch next month for the following absorbing stories:

PRACTICE MAKES MARRIAGE	Marion Lennox
LOVING REMEDY	Joanna Neil
CRISIS POINT	Grace Read
A SUBTLE MAGIC	Meredith Webber